Hitched to a Star

Hitched to a Star

by

Bernard Palmer

MOODY PRESS
CHICAGO

© 1981 by
MOODY BIBLE INSTITUTE
CHICAGO, ILLINOIS

Library of Congress Cataloging in Publication Data

Palmer, Bernard Alvin, 1914—
   Hitched to a star.

   Summary: A fourteen-year-old suppresses much of his own per-
sonality in order to stay in step with his older brother who is a
gifted athlete, a born leader, and a dedicated Christian.
   [1. Christian life—Fiction.   2. Brothers and sisters—
Fiction.   3. Family life—Fiction]
I. Title.
PZ7.P183Hi   (Fic)   81-9636
ISBN 0-8024-3584-X   AACR2

Printed in the United States of America

1

Fourteen-year-old Russ Masters took the snap from his older brother and faded to the edge of the lawn behind him. He pictured a wild, clawing trio of giants in shoulder pads and helmets charging through the line. Scrambling to avoid the imaginary tacklers, he gave Chuck time to dash to the other side of the lawn. As his brother veered sharply to the right, Russ fired the pigskin in a wobbly, uncertain, high-scoring arc. It was overthrown and wide, but Chuck drifted effortlessly to his left and leaped high to haul it in.

"How was that?" Russ called as the star Platte Valley High quarterback came down with the ball.

Chuck tossed it a few feet in the air and caught it. "Better."

The younger boy wiped his hands on the sides of his jeans and sauntered forward, frustration darkening his rugged young features. "Don't con me, Chuck," he retorted. "That pass was lousy."

Chuck palmed the pigskin expertly and moved toward his brother with a confident, casual stride. He was taller than Russ by half a head, and powerfully built. Already he had the thick neck and muscular arms and legs of a well-developed athlete.

"It wasn't so good," he acknowledged, his grin taking much of the sting from his words. "But it's not the worst pass I've seen you uncork, and that's the truth. You're comin' great for your age, Russ. All you've got to do is keep at it."

Russ glanced at the sprawling brick ranch house where he and Chuck lived with their parents. The dying sun was reflecting off the broad picture window in the living room overlooking the front yard. He was glad his dad was not home yet. He would be standing behind the thermopane thinking how clumsy his younger son was.

His dad had never *said* he was clumsy, that he knew of, but Russ knew that was what he was thinking. He saw how proud Mr. Masters was every time Chuck connected with a touchdown pass. And he saw how avidly his folks clipped the stories of Chuck's exploits from the local paper.

There was not any use in his trying. He would never make a football player. He would never do *anything* to make his folks proud of him. Not like they were proud of Chuck.

He ran his stubby fingers through his heavy shock of sandy hair. That hair was the only thing about him that was anything like his illustrious older brother, and it sure did not do much good when it came to playing football.

"You can't expect to handle the ball the way I—the way the guys on the varsity do," Chuck said, reassuringly.

That was a laugh! Russ told himself. He would never be able to make it on the football field in a hundred years. Not the way Chuck had.

He did not know why, but just about everybody in town thought he was going to be a football great because his name was Masters, too. "We'll burn up the conference the next few years," men would say to each other when they got to

8

talking high school football, which was the chief subject every fall. "We've got Chuck Masters running the team now, and that kid brother of his is coming along when he graduates."

"Yep. Have you seen Russ lately? He's a ringer for Chuck, except that he's lighter by forty pounds. But he's young and he's growing."

Russ did not think he looked all that much like his handsome, talented brother. His nose was too large, for one thing, and his lips were thin and pinched. And he was sure that he would never be as big as Chuck. Still, he was flattered when someone told him that he looked like his brother. If only they did not expect him to play football as well.

When Russ first went to junior high nobody paid much attention to him on the football field, but that was because Chuck had only been a promise then—a bright prospect for the future. When the older Masters boy burst into prominence, people suddenly discovered Russ. It was not long until they began to hope openly that the second Masters would be as outstanding as the first.

The comparison terrified Russ. When he did not measure up to Chuck they would blame him for it. He could not figure out why they expected so much of him. They should have known better. By the time his older brother had been fourteen their mom had filled a scrapbook with newspaper clippings about his prowess on the gridiron.

MASTERS, the headlines shouted. MASTERS. MASTERS. MASTERS! It was not long until everybody in town was talking about Chuck. Half the time the reporter did not bother to use the boy's first name, and Russ knew why. There was no need for it. Chuck was the only Masters in school who was doing anything worthy of being mentioned in the paper. The only real claim Russ had to recognition was that he had been born Chuck's younger brother.

It was not that Russ did not love Chuck. He could not have had a finer, more wonderful older brother, or one he thought more of. Yet there were times he was under such pressure because of his older brother that he wished he had never heard of anyone by the name of Chuck Masters.

He was still motionless on the lawn when their father approached the drive, coming home from his office in town.

"Show Dad how well you can do!" Chuck called out.

Russ groaned silently. That was the last thing he wanted to do right then. How could he let his dad see how terrible he was?

Mr. Masters waved to his sons and stopped on the cement approach to the two-car garage.

"Watch Russ, Dad!"

"Let 'er rip!"

Numbly the younger boy took his place a dozen feet or so behind Chuck. Why did he have to have an older brother who could do everything?

"Ready?" his brother asked.

"I—I guess so."

The older boy shot the ball to him and raced forward, using the same pattern as before. Russ faded back and rifled it into the flat ten or twelve yards beyond the mythical line of scrimmage. It was not a long pass, but it was well thrown.

"Not bad!" Mr. Masters said. "Not bad!" The younger boy smiled, and for an instant he felt the warm glow of approval.

"That was a good pass, Russ. You're doin' great!"

Scuffing the grass with a toe, he frowned uneasily. He

did feel good about his father's praise, but it bothered him as well. One decent pass and both Dad and Chuck were turning handsprings. That only showed how clumsily he threw most of the time.

While Chuck waited for him to get set, Russ lifted his gaze to look beyond his football-playing brother. A row of towering Australian pines marked the southern limits of the Masters' country acreage. Across the wide pasture was the farmstead where the new neighbors lived. The Varner barn housed some of the best quarter horses in the state of Nebraska, according to the people around town.

Russ had been admiring the herd of sleek mares and geldings that usually grazed in the pasture near the highway. Someday he was going over and see the rest of the Varner quarter horse stock and get acquainted with the farmer who owned them. If he were doing what he really wanted to, he would be riding a horse right then, instead of doing such a miserable job of throwing a football.

"Hurry it up, Russ!" Chuck called to him.

Grimly he forced thoughts of the horses aside and moved mechanically into position. Someday he might be able to make his dad as proud of him as he was of Chuck.

Crouching to take the ball, he shivered in his light jacket and slapped his hands together. It had been warm that late October afternoon when they got home from school. Now the sun was slipping behind the distant hills, and there was a bite to the wind that swirled the leaves along the ground. A Russian thistle, brown and dry as the corn in the fields, broke free of its mooring and went bounding over the lawn, sowing its noxious seeds with abandon.

The wind had an effect on his throwing, and the next two passes were wide of the mark. Still, his older brother man-

11

aged to scamper across the grass and spear them. Before the boys could try again, Mrs. Masters rang the bell outside the kitchen door to signal that dinner was ready and it was time for them to go in.

Russ carried the ball into the house, put it in the closet at the far end of the hall, and went into the bathroom to wash up. For a moment he studied the reflection of his serious young face in the mirror. As he had been going through the family room just then, he had seen the paper his father was reading. It was a day-old Omaha *World-Herald* turned to the sports section. The reporter gave a report on Platte Valley's coming game with the leading conference contender from the eastern part of the state. The kids at school had been talking about the same story that morning.

"Chuck's the best quarterback anyone in the league has ever seen. And that's a fact!" one of Russ's friends remarked.

"Yeah. In a few years he'll be playin' with the Broncos."

Russ was proud to be Chuck's brother. There was no denying that. And why wouldn't he be? As the guys said, Chuck was the best quarterback who had ever played football at Platte Valley. If it just were not so hard for him! Chuck's was a tough act to follow.

"We were about to eat without you," Mr. Masters told him.

He pulled out a chair and dropped into it.

"You were looking good out there, son."

"Thanks." He could not help wondering if his dad really meant it or if he was just trying to make him feel good.

"Keep it up and you'll be quarterbacking the varsity in a couple of years."

Russ glanced up. The warmth he had felt suddenly iced.

There it was again. His dad was expecting him to be like Chuck. Like Chuck. Like Chuck.

"Don't hold your breath," he muttered bleakly.

"I mean it. You were doing fine out there tonight." Then he turned his attention to his oldest son, asking about the varsity practice.

During the meal Chuck and Mr. Masters discussed the preparations for the game with Sidley the following night. Russ was surprised to learn that his dad knew most of the Sidley starting offensive and defensive lineups by name and was able to talk about their strengths and weaknesses as thoroughly as though he had scouted them himself. Russ listened in silence. There was nothing he could add that would even have made sense.

Presently his older brother glanced at the clock on the mantel in the living room and then at his watch. "I've got to get going. I've got a couple of meetings at church."

"You'll be in early, won't you?" his mother asked.

"He'd better be," Mr. Masters broke in. He turned to Chuck. "I wanted to talk to you about that. You were out later than you should have been last night. If you're going to be ready for the big game tomorrow night, you've got to get your rest."

"It shouldn't be late," Chuck told him. He started out, but came back into the room a pace or two. "How about it, Russ?" he asked. "Want to go along?"

The younger boy shook his head. He did not say anything about it around home—it would only make for a hassle if he did—but he did not go for all that church stuff Chuck and his folks were so involved in. He had prayed and prayed that God would help him play football well enough so his dad would be proud of him, but it had not done any good. The

13

way Russ looked at it, if God could not take care of a thing like that, He could not do much for a guy.

"Can't make it tonight," he told his brother lamely.

"We could sure use you in the choir. It only lasts an hour." Chuck paused for a moment. "I could kick out of the committee meeting early enough to get back here and pick you up."

"I've got to study," Russ said curtly.

His brother's smile flashed. "Maybe next time."

"Yeah, maybe next time." But they both knew that he really did not mean it. It was only a way of getting off an unpleasant subject.

2

When Chuck had gone Mr. Masters wandered into the family room, sought his favorite chair in front of the fireplace, and picked up the newspaper. Idly he turned to an inner page in the sports section and had just begun to read when his younger son came to the door. Russ's hazel eyes were fixed, uncertainly, on his dad.

The boy had been waiting almost a week for the right occasion to talk to him. Now time had almost run out. If he was going to be able to go to the horse sale Saturday night, he had to know.

He had been wanting a horse for as long as he could remember. And for almost that long his father had been promising one. "Dad," he said, clearing his throat, uneasily.

Mr. Masters looked up. For a brief instant irritation marred his features. "Yes, Russ?"

"I've got something I—I'd like to talk to you about," he began uncertainly. He did not know why, but the last few months he had been increasingly uncomfortable around his father. He could not talk with him the way Chuck did, or even the way he used to.

"Fine." Mr. Masters folded the paper and put it aside. "I was just reading about Chuck in the Omaha paper."

He felt the crimson steal up his throat and spread into his cheeks.

"We can all be proud of that brother of yours. If he doesn't get hurt, he'll make a name for himself as a Cornhusker. I look for him to make the pros." He paused significantly. "Wouldn't it be great if he'd be drafted as the Denver Broncos' quarterback?"

Russ tried to sound excited about the prospect, but his words were flat and wooden, as though they came from deep inside some distant cave.

"I was glad to see you and Chuck workin' out this afternoon. You're doing OK, but you've got to hang in there every day if you expect to take over Chuck's job as quarterback when he graduates."

The younger boy squirmed uncomfortably.

His dad read the uneasiness on his face and changed the subject. "What was it you wanted to talk to me about?"

"I don't have to see you right now," he said, swallowing hard. "I can wait until later."

"We'll talk about it now, Russ," Mr. Masters said firmly. "What's on your mind?"

The boy cleared his throat. Getting started was the most difficult part. He knew what he wanted to say, but now that he was actually facing his dad the words stuck in his throat.

"I—I've been thinking," he began at last, "that I—I'd like to get that horse you promised me." There! It was out! He had actually said it. Russ studied his dad's lean face anxiously.

"Did I do a foolish thing like that?"

The boy hitched his chair closer and leaned forward intently. "Don't you remember?" he asked, his voice bleak and apprehensive.

16

"Did I promise to get you a horse?"

"I—I—" Russ began. Then he saw the faint smile gleaming in his father's dark eyes and hope surged within him.

"Seriously, Russ," he said, "I've thought about it, but not for the last six months or so. And I'm sorry about that. Why didn't you remind me?"

"I did," he replied. "I mean I tried to remind you, but—" He was about to tell his dad that he had not had a chance to talk to him about what he wanted because Mr. Masters had been too busy with Chuck's athletic activities. But he could not do that.

"I made you a promise, and I intend to keep it."

The words sank slowly into the boy's consciousness.

"I—I—" His voice was robbed of words and remorse swept over him in a sudden, chilling wave. He had convinced himself that his father would find some reason to refuse him. He had steeled himself against that happening, but he had been wrong. He was going to get the horse he had wanted for so long!

"Of course we'll have to find a place to keep the horse until we get a barn built," Mr. Masters continued. "Why don't you snoop around and see what you can come up with?"

Russ beamed. He was going to have a horse of his own. It was actually happening! "There's this quarter horse sale coming up Saturday night," he said, thrusting a sale bill into his father's hands. "There ought to be some great quarter horses sold."

"There's no use in my looking at this list," he said, handing it back to his son. "I don't know a thing about quarter horses."

Russ had not reached the place yet where he had even thought about that. All his concern had been centered around getting permission from his dad to get a horse. He had heard some of his friends talking about bloodlines, but he did not know anything about it himself.

"I think maybe our new neighbor could help you, Russ," his dad suggested. "Why don't you go over and see him?"

"I don't know him, Dad," he protested.

"He's a nice guy, and probably one of the most knowledgeable horsemen in this part of the state. I'm sure he could give you some valuable advice."

"That's a good idea." He got to his feet. "Want to go with me to talk to him?"

"Sorry, Russ," Mr. Masters said, smiling. "I've got some work to take care of so I can go to the game tomorrow night. You wouldn't want me to miss that, would you?"

A faint shadow crept over the bright new sun that had suddenly shone in the boy's life. Then it passed as suddenly as it came. He was going to get his horse! After all those months and years of waiting. And not just *any* horse. He was going to get a quarter horse, the most popular breed in the ranch country.

He could not wait until the next day to seek out their neighbor's advice. He got permission to go to the Varner farm, put on his jacket, and slipped out into the bracing night air. The moon was riding high, spreading its cold light across the pasture and the cluster of buildings beyond. Every detail of the farmstead stood out in bold relief. The house was larger than his parents' home, and smoke from the fireplace stabbed a gray finger to the sky. To his left the horses were grazing quietly near the big windmill-fed tank, and the handful of spring colts were running about in gay abandon.

18

He slipped through the fence and hurried across the uneven ground, clutching the sale bill in his slim fingers. Maybe he would get a mare so he could raise a colt. He could have a new colt every year, and by the time he was out of college he would have a nucleus of a herd of horses—a start in the quarter-horse business.

He might even be able to get a job at the Varner place so he could find out as much as possible about training and raising horses. Just being with a man like that would be great. In the length of time it took to cross the pasture he had decided that he would work almost for free, just to have the chance to learn.

The Varner German shepherd lustily announced Russ's presence. The dog, with the hair on the back of his neck bristling, blocked his path to the front gate. Russ stopped uncertainly. At that instant the kitchen door flew open.

"Duke!" a familiar young voice sang out. "Come here!"

Reluctantly the dog backed off, a step at a time.

"He won't hurt you," the voice told Russ.

Still he hesitated. "Are you sure?"

He looked up from the dog to the owner of the voice. He guessed he had known Dianne Varner lived there. She was in his English class at school. He had been so disturbed by Duke's belligerence, however, that he had completely forgotten about her until that moment. Her slim form moved to one side, and she grasped the big animal by the collar and guided him into the kitchen where he planted himself, protectively, beside her.

"That's a good dog," she murmured.

She was motionless in the doorway. The light behind her cast an auburn halo about her head, and in the dim shadows Russ could make out her delicate features and quick smile.

19

She was wearing a light yellow sweater with a high neck, a pair of faded, patched jeans, and cowboy boots.

"I thought that was you, Russ," Dianne said, warmly. "Come on in."

Even then he did not move immediately. "Are you sure it's all right?" he asked, still eyeing the dog.

"Of course."

"I know that," he told her, "and you know it, but does Duke know it?"

Her laughter trilled. "As long as you don't make any quick moves toward Mother or me, he'll be your friend." She held the door open wide for him.

"You'll tell him we're friends, won't you?"

At that moment a pleasant voice called from another part of the house. "Who is it, Dianne?"

"One of the boys from school," she answered. "Russ Masters."

Russ stood just inside the kitchen door, shifting his weight from one foot to the other. "I—I came over to see your dad."

"I'm sorry. He won't be back until Wednesday."

Russ Masters's smile fled.

"Is there something wrong?" she asked, noting the concern in his eyes.

There was a sound at the archway that led to the living room, and he looked up to see a plump, friendly woman about the age of his mother. Her hair was the color of Dianne's, and her features had the same finely chiseled look. He was startled, however, to see that she was in a wheelchair.

When she greeted him her voice was gay; not at all what he would have expected from one who was unable to walk.

20

"Maybe there is something we could do for you," she said when she learned the reason for his visit. "Both Dianne and I have been involved with quarter horses for a long time. We could check the bloodlines for you, if that's what you want."

Mrs. Varner wheeled herself into the kitchen, and Dianne pulled up a straight-backed chair beside her. They had also received a sale bill and had already glanced at it, but now they studied it seriously.

"As many horses as there are on this list," Dianne said, "there ought to be several that would suit your purpose." She paused. "Of course we couldn't be absolutely sure until we've checked their bloodlines in the register and have looked them over for conformation."

He eyed her blankly. "And where do I get a copy of the quarter horse registry?" he asked.

"We've got one."

He was going to ask if they would loan it to him, but Mrs. Varner anticipated the question and told him that borrowing the big book would not do him much good. "In order to use the registry properly you have to know something about bloodlines. It tells the ancestry of each horse registered, but that's all."

He had not known buying a quarter horse would be so complicated. Of course, that had been the reason his dad suggested that he come over to see Mr. Varner.

"Dianne has been helping her dad for the last two or three years," her mother said. "She could go over the sale bill with you, check out the horses that seem promising, and even go to the sale with you Saturday night."

"Hey, that'd be great!" Then he glanced quickly at her, as though he just realized she might refuse. "OK?"

Her smile agreed.

"And now," Mrs. Varner said, "we'll have some hot chocolate." She gave the wheel a vigorous push with her hand and glided over to the refrigerator.

3

The following morning Russ sought out Dianne Varner as soon as he and Chuck got to school. She must have arrived only moments before, for she was putting her jacket in her locker when he came up.

She was several inches shorter than he, as slim and lithe as a cottonwood sapling along the lazy Platte River. Her copper hair was long and flowed over her shoulders, framing her nut-brown features and quick smile. It was obvious that she was born to the out-of-doors. She was probably more at home on a horse than inside sewing or doing housework.

"Hi," he said.

Her smile flashed in response. "I was just going to look for you."

"And I saved you the trouble. Wasn't that nice of me?"

They walked down the hall together.

"There are some good horses on that bill."

"That's great!" His eyes brightened. "Find anything that would be good for Dad and me to look at?"

"I think so." He expected her to go on, but instead she glanced at her watch. "But I don't have time to go into it right now."

"Maybe we can get together at noon," he said, hopefully.

"Sounds like a good idea. I'll meet you in the lunch room. OK?"

Talking with her in the hall was one thing, but sitting with her was something else. He was not too keen on it, in spite of the fact that he had suggested it. He knew what the guys would say when they found out.

When the final period of the morning was over he scurried out of class as quickly as possible, trying to melt into the crowd before Grant and Mel spied him, but that was not to be.

"Hey!" one of them called, "wait up!"

He pretended not to hear his friend, but Mel pushed his way through the crowd and grasped him by the arm. "Russ! Remember us?"

He grinned sheepishly.

"What're you tryin' to do?" his friend demanded. "Sneak off?"

"Who, me?"

Mel nodded.

"What makes you think I'd do that?"

By this time Grant had joined them. "Come on, Russ!" he said. "Who're you eatin' lunch with?"

Russ's cheeks burned and he looked away, but not quickly enough. His friends noticed it and laughed boisterously.

"Lay off, will you?"

"Who is she?"

"Listen, you apes! You've got it all wrong!"

They threw back their heads and laughed.

Dianne chose that moment to appear. She came breezing

24

up to Russ out of the surging crowd. "I've been looking all over for you!"

Mel poked him in the ribs and grinned widely. Russ's cheeks crimsoned, and he looked quickly away. Grant, who was standing on the other side, had that same impish gleam in his eyes. "So long," he murmured. With that his two friends swaggered to a table nearby, where Russ would be sure to see them every time he looked up.

He did not think he had ever been so embarrassed in all his life. The worst of it was, they would never believe that he was seeing Dianne on business.

She did not seem to notice Grant and Mel. She opened her English book and took out the sale bill. "Mom and I found eight horses that were worth checking, and three or four of those have bloodlines you might be interested in."

"Great!" His voice raised, and Mel snickered audibly.

Dianne looked up, and then directed her attention back to him. By this time his left eye was twitching nervously. Wait till he got those characters alone! He would strangle them both with his bare hands.

"But," she continued, "if I were buying for myself, I would look at this gelding first. He's out of a strong, intelligent line."

"Great!"

"And, according to the sale bill," she said, "he's broke to ride and has been started on roping, barrel racing, and cutting cattle."

He grinned his appreciation in spite of the fact that his friends were watching with obvious delight. "That sounds better all the time. Man, you know *everything* there is to know about quarter horses."

Dianne seemed embarrassed by the compliment. "I was just reading what it says on the sale bill."

"You didn't find everything you've told me about that horse's background on the sale bill!" he protested.

"Don't thank me for anything I've told you about his bloodlines. Thank Mom. She's the one who spends hours pouring over the quarter horse books."

"She's the greatest—" He thought about her handicap and the fact that she was cheerful and completely lacking in self-pity. He had never known anyone quite like her. "How did it happen?" he asked, curious. "Why is she in a wheelchair?"

"She was thrown by a horse a few years ago—when I was just a little girl and —" She gestured helplessly.

He wanted to say something about her mother, expressing his sympathy, but he could not find words for it. All he could think of was his own mother and how terrible it would be to have her crippled.

For an instant concern and self-pity flooded Dianne's delicate young features. Then she shook herself and smiled.

"What do you think about those horses, Russ?" she asked, jerking him back to reality. "Are there any that excite you?"

"The gelding sounds really good."

"You'll have to look him over carefully," she warned, "to be sure that he measures up to his bloodlines."

"That's one of our problems. Neither Dad or I know anything about judging a horses's conformation."

Dianne hesitated. "I don't know if I could help," she said, "but if you want me to, I'll go to the sale and look him over for you."

"Hey, that's super!"

She smiled.

Russ could scarcely wait to get home that afternoon to tell his dad that Dianne had agreed to go to the sale with them. He burst into the house after school and called out to his mother. "When will Dad be home?"

"I don't know," she answered.

He rushed to the kitchen to tell her about his conversation with Dianne that noon. He was so excited the words tumbled out.

". . . and she really knows horses!" he concluded.

"That's nice," his mother replied, casually, as though he had made a remark about the weather or a good grade he had received on an English paper. It was useless to try to talk to her about the horse he wanted to get. She would not really hear what he was saying.

Russ pulled up a chair and sat down at the kitchen table.

"Dad ought to be home before long," she said presently, glancing at the clock. "He's never late on game nights."

Game night! A chill swept over him. He had forgotten all about that. There was no use trying to talk with his father, either, until the next day. He would be as hard to get through to as Mrs. Masters had been. Russ's shoulders sagged, and he laid the half-eaten cracker on the table.

"Is there something wrong?" his mother asked.

He shook his head.

"What is it?" she persisted.

"Nothing, Mom."

His dad came home from the office half an hour early, changed into heavy clothes against the bite of the mid-October wind and ate hurriedly. Shortly after 6:30 the family left for the game.

Platte Valley won the toss, and on the first series of

downs Chuck sparked his team's offensive play. He whipped the ball to the tight end for a six-yard gain and on the second play sent the running back through a hole off-tackle that gave them five yards and a first-and-ten. The next play was an incomplete pass, but Chuck called the pattern again. The receiver drew it in and scampered fourteen yards for another first down.

By that time Platte Valley was on the march. With an unerring sense of timing Chuck mixed running plays with passing to keep the drive on the move. They plunged across the 50-yard line to Sidley's 40. Then the youthful quarterback hurled a bulletlike pass the receiver scooped up inches above the ground and would have scored had he not stumbled on the 3. Before the opposition knew what was happening, Platte Valley was on the board for seven points.

Stunned by the quick score, Sidley received the ball, clawing for revenge. They marched to the Platte Valley 12 before a fumble stopped them. But they were not defeated yet. They had earned their number two rating in the state against Platte Valley's sixth place and were determined to prove that they were worthy of it. They forced Chuck and his teammates to punt and then launched another drive themselves that ended with a field goal.

Midway in the second quarter Sidley scored again and made the extra point to forge ahead, 10 to 7. There the score stood until the dying moments of the game when Chuck uncorked a dazzling pass that caught Sidley flat-footed and gave Platte Valley another six points. They missed the kick, but the way things worked out, they did not need it. The final score was 10-13.

The local crowd went wild as they piled out of the stands and made for their cars. Russ was among them. In a way he

28

was glad he had come with his folks and had to wait until they returned to the car to leave the parking lot. It gave him more opportunity to meet people and have them talk with him about the game and the tremendous job of quarterbacking Chuck had done.

Although the game had been exhilerating, his thoughts drifted to the horse sale. Two or three times he tried to tell his dad about the horse Dianne and her mother had suggested they bid on, but it was no use. All Mr. Masters could think or talk about was the game. Exasperated, Russ sat back and listened.

He was sure his father had completely forgotten what they were to do the following night. He had decided that something was sure to happen to keep them away. He wanted a horse so badly he could not accept the fact that he was actually about to get one—and a pure-bred quarter horse at that. The next morning, however, the first thing his dad asked about was the time they would have to leave the house to get out to the sale barn.

Russ eyed him happily. He had not expected anything like that. He had felt all along that his dad really did not want to get him a horse. Now he had to change his mind.

For the second night running the Masters family had dinner earlier than usual. As soon as they finished, Russ and his dad drove to the Varner place, where they picked up Dianne, and went out to the sale barn.

They could have located the three-year-old gelding Dianne and her mother picked out without the identifying number on his back. He was stocky and powerfully built, with a broad chest and heavily muscled legs, the sort of horse that could run all day without tiring. His coat was a shining black with a scattering of white hairs dusted across his neck and withers, like Russ's mother, who had begun to gray before her time. There was a certain pride in his stature, as though he knew already how much he pleased them.

Mr. Masters hesitated briefly before moving forward to take a closer look. "There is something striking about him," he said. "I don't know much about horses, but this one's sure a beauty."

Russ beamed.

But there was still another problem standing between him and ownership of the magnificent young animal. He watched fearfully as other prospective buyers came by, studying the sleek black gelding the way Dianne had. It was no use, he told himself miserably, his spirits sagging. The horse was too outstanding for him. There would be too many bidders running up the price. Mr. Masters would not be able to get the gelding.

The auctioneer started the sale on time in spite of the fact that the crowd was slow in arriving. And, strangely enough, the horse Russ was interested in was among the first to be sold.

Dianne's eyes brightened as she heard the gelding's number called and the auctioneer began to read his bloodlines. She leaned toward Russ. "That's good," she said. "That's very good. He's being sold early. Before a lot of the out-of-town buyers arrive."

While Russ twisted nervously, the auctioneer began his chant. There were only two other bidders and one of them dropped out early. After a few minutes the other potential buyer quit, too, and the auctioneer knocked off the horse to Mr. Masters.

Russ turned wordlessly to Dianne. He wanted to thank

her, but could not trust himself to speak. He had a horse of his own. He actually owned a horse! After all this time! His throat choked, and he looked away.

"I'm so happy for you," she murmured.

4

Another horse was led into the ring, and the sale continued, but Russ had suddenly lost interest. He left his father and Dianne in the stands and made his way to the place where his new horse was tethered. He was so engrossed in the beautiful young animal he did not even realize that he had left his companions.

A warm glow spread over him as he stopped a few feet from the powerfully built young gelding. He had a horse of his own. It still did not seem possible.

The huge double doors at the far end of the barn were open. He could feel the cool kiss of the wind against his cheek and his nostrils picked up the pungent odor of horses in the long line of stalls.

"There, boy," he said, softly, reaching out to lay his hand on the three-year-old's broad back.

"Easy. Easy."

Black ears went up and the head came around quickly. Russ could feel the gelding's skin tremble beneath his hand.

"Easy, boy."

His fingers found the horse's soft muzzle, and he stroked him with a gentle touch. "You and I are goin' to have big times together," he murmured.

"I'd be proud of him too, Russ," a soft voice said from behind him. "He's beautiful."

Only then did Russ realize that Dianne and his dad had followed him. "Hi," he said, grinning, self-consciously. In that instant he felt a closeness to his father that he had not known in the last year or two.

"We'd better get this horse to wherever you're going to keep him, Russ," Mr. Masters said. "Dianne volunteered her dad's horse trailer."

Russ stared numbly. "What did you say?"

"You found a place to keep the horse, didn't you?"

"Me?" the boy repeated. "I thought you were going to do that."

"When you first talked to me about coming to this sale, I told you that you would have to find a place to keep a horse, until we could get something built. Remember?"

Russ groaned. He had been so caught up in the excitement of talking with Dianne about bloodlines and choosing the right horse from the sale bill that he had completely forgotten he was supposed to find a place to keep the horse for a while.

"Oh, man!" he exclaimed. "What do we do now?"

Mr. Masters tensed. Russ saw his reaction and cringed inwardly.

"That's your problem, son. As badly as you wanted a horse, I didn't think you'd forget the most important element of the whole arrangement."

"Do you suppose we could keep him out here for a few days?" the boy asked in desperation.

"No way. There's no one here to take care of him. You're going to have to come up with something better than that."

"We've got room," Dianne broke in.

"Are you sure?" Mr. Masters asked.

"I'd have to talk to Mom first, but I'm sure she and Dad wouldn't care if you bring your new horse over to our place, at least until you make some other arrangements."

Russ's dad drove out to the Varner place and went inside with Dianne and his son to talk to Mrs. Varner about keeping the horse on their farm. She was not sure her husband would want to board the animal indefinitely, she said, but she knew he would not mind having the gelding around until they found another place to keep him. And, as Dianne had said, it was all right for them to use the Varner horse trailer.

"Want me to go to the sale barn with you and help load him?" Dianne asked.

Russ hesitated. He liked the idea of having her along, but he did not know what his dad and Chuck would say about it. He was afraid they would tease him later, when they were alone with him.

"I think we'd both appreciate your help," Mr. Masters told her, a crooked grin twisting his lips. "Neither Russ or I are what you would call experts when it comes to handling horses."

"We could probably manage."

"Maybe we can," Mr. Masters told him, "but there are a lot of things I'd rather do than spend half of Saturday night getting a horse into a trailer. Especially when we've got somebody who knows how to go with us."

"Fine," Dianne said, getting in the front seat and scooting to the center so Russ could sit beside her. He paused briefly, debating whether to get in front or to separate himself from Dianne by crawling into the back seat. While he fumbled uncertainly with his decision, his dad decided for him.

34

"Come on, Russ," he chided. "Let's get this show on the road."

"Right!" He got in front and closed the door behind him.

Others were milling around the barn when they got back, looking over the horses yet to be sold or waiting for an opportunity to load their own purchases and head for home. Mr. Masters backed the trailer into position near a side door and opened the tailgate to form a ramp. Russ went into the big barn, loosed the halter rope that held his horse in the stall, and led him out into the chill night air. The gelding was tense, fiddlefooting nervously. He jerked his head, and the boy tightened his grip on the short rope.

"Easy now!" he exclaimed under his breath. "Easy!"

The frightened animal braced his feet, nostrils flaring. The harder Russ pulled, the more the powerful young gelding resisted. If he was not careful, he reasoned, uneasily, everybody at the sale would soon know how inexperienced he was.

"The horse is frightened," Dianne explained, quietly. "Too many strange things have happened to him."

When she reached for the rope he let her take it. Briefly she talked to the frightened quarter horse until his head came down slightly and his eyes narrowed—indications that his terror was subsiding. Once she had him quieted, Dianne moved closer to take the halter from her free hand. Talking softly she started toward the trailer and he went along. Once his front feet were on the trailer ramp, he stopped and jerked his head, his ears twitching.

"Easy, boy," she murmured reassuringly. Then, tightening her grip she stepped forward. An instant later he was inside.

"Thanks!" Mr. Masters said. "I don't think Russ and I could have managed him."

"Actually," she said, "he wasn't all that hard to load."

After they got the chunky three-year-old out of the trailer, Russ and his father thanked Dianne again.

"Come over tomorrow, Russ," she told him, "and see how he's doing. OK?"

"I'll do that." In fact, he was so excited he did not know how he could stay away.

"She's a nice girl, Russ," his dad said as they drove home. "And she sure knows her horses."

His son agreed completely with him, but did not reply.

The next afternoon when dinner was over Russ Masters rode his bike to the Varner place. He started directly for the barn, but decided that he had better let Dianne know he was there, so he went up on the kitchen porch and knocked briskly. Through the glass he could see that a lamp was on in the living room and thin, gray smoke curled upward from the fireplace chimney, warm and inviting.

He knocked a second time. At first all was silent. Then a savage growl rumbled from somewhere inside the house. Duke! He had forgotten all about the big dog! Russ took half a step backward. Almost at that instant wild barking filled the air, and the door rattled noisily on its hinges as the huge German shepherd lunged against it.

The boy leaped backward off the porch. He stumbled and almost fell in his haste to put some distance between himself and the angry dog.

"Duke!" Dianne shouted from the barn.

It was as though the police dog had not even heard her above the din he was making. His young mistress called to him again, sternly. Whether he heard then or realized the suspected intruder had backed away, Russ did not know. All he was aware of was that the dog had fallen silent. Still he did not move closer to the house, but turned to face Dianne as she came up beside him. In spite of himself his heart hammered against his rib cage.

"I thought I was a goner."

"Duke's very protective of Mother and me—especially when Dad is away."

Russ shuddered. "Your dad's not going to have to worry about anyone bothering the place."

They went into the barn together.

"I decided to curry him, Russ," she said. "I hope you don't mind."

He glanced at her. She was the only person he knew who loved horses so much she would curry one that did not even belong to her. "Oh, no," he said quickly. "I don't mind. Thanks." At the stall where his gelding was tied, he paused. "Thought I'd come over and take another look at Dusty."

"That's a nice name."

"It's on his registration certificate. Gentleman Joe's Dusty."

She picked up the currycomb and brush and handed them to Russ. He set to work, taking up where Dianne left off, currying and brushing his new horse until Dusty's sleek coat gleamed.

"You're going to talk to Dad about keeping him until you get a place built, aren't you?" she asked, presently.

He nodded. "Of course, you've got a lot of horses around. Your dad may figure he doesn't have room for another one."

Lee Varner got home late Tuesday evening. The next afternoon when school was out Russ went over to see him about keeping Dusty at his place. Mr. Varner had been expecting him.

"Dianne showed me your horse this morning."

Russ waited uneasily.

"You've got yourself a fine animal. Train him right, and he'll be all you'll ever want in a quarter horse."

"Do—do you think I can keep him here until we get a stable built?"

Mr. Varner hesitated, his pale blue eyes narrowing. "That depends. I've been looking for someone to help around here. Would you be interested?"

The boy faltered. That was more than he could have hoped for, but there was one drawback. "I'm still in school."

Mr. Varner brushed the dust from his handmade boots. "You could work on Saturdays, couldn't you?" he asked. "And after school when I need you?"

Russ stared at Dianne's father. There had to be some mistake. He could not be fortunate enough to get a job with one of the finest quarter horse breeders in the state. "Sure—Sure. I can help you."

"That's settled, then. I'll take the care of your horse out of your wages. OK?"

Russ Masters went home as though in a dream. He not only had a place for Dusty, but he also had a job, and he could learn all about quarter horses and their bloodlines.

38

5

Russ hurried home from school the day after making arrangements with Mr. Varner to keep Dusty at his place. He changed clothes hurriedly and ran across the pasture, heading straight for the barn. He did not think it necessary to tell anyone what he was doing. He worked there now. He had a right to be there.

He got a small pail of oats to use in enticing Dusty to leave the other horses and approach him, then slipped between the wires and made his way toward the gelding. The proud young horse lifted his head, ears twitching, as Russ called him by name.

The boy moved forward a step or two at a time, hesitantly, extending the pail of oats. The bridle in his left hand was hidden from the wary horse. The muscles under the gelding's gleaming black hair quivered, and Russ sensed the mounting tension. He waited patiently, his voice calm and soothing. Not until Dusty began to relax did he move forward again.

It took another minute or two for the distance between the boy and his horse to vanish. Dusty's nostrils flared and his head jerked—but only for an instant. Russ tightened his grip and forced the bit into the gelding's mouth.

Once the bridle strap was fastened the three-year-old relaxed, and Russ led him into the corral. He tied him to the fence while he went for the saddle. Moments later he was ready to climb aboard Dusty and ride out to look at the rest of the horses.

He was mounting Dusty when Dianne came charging around the corner of the barn on her horse, Shadow. Startled, his horse reared, and it was all he could do to find the stirrup with his right foot and remain in the saddle.

"Hi!" she cried, reining to a halt a few feet away. "I figured you'd be over to do some riding today."

"For a couple of minutes I thought this was one ride that would end with me on my back in the grass."

They went off together at a leisurely gait. "I found out that I could stay with him. And for me, that was something."

"You ride very well," she assured him.

He glanced quizzically in her direction, trying to decide whether she meant what she said or was taunting him. It did not seem like her to ridicule a friend, but he was so uncomfortable in the saddle that afternoon, he could not be sure.

On Saturday Russ was at the Varner place a few minutes before eight, ready to go to work. Dianne's dad had him saddle Dusty and ride fence. If any of the barbed wire was down he was to make what repairs he could. If he could not do them, he was to come back for help.

He discovered that the fences were in good repair, except for two or three places where the wire sagged because the staples had been pulled out. He was able to fix them all without difficulty. Mr. Varner only grunted when Russ told him what he had done, but the boy thought he saw approval in the rancher's brown eyes.

In the afternoon Russ helped Mr. Varner move hay from one of the outlying fields to the barn. It was a sweaty, back-breaking job, and Russ thought quitting time would never come. When they finally knocked off work he was so exhausted he almost went to sleep at the dinner table.

Raising quarter horses had always sounded intriguing, he told himself as he lay in bed that night, staring blankly up at the ceiling. He was beginning to realize that there was a great deal of hard, wearisome work involved—more than he could ever have supposed. They would be hauling hay until freeze up, along with cleaning out the barns, currying and combing the show horses, and helping train the green-broke colts. At that point it seemed to Russ that everything about raising horses was difficult. He knew now that he was going to have to work hard if he was ever to accomplish anything in that field.

During the next few weeks, until it got too cold, Russ saddled Dusty and went for a ride at every opportunity. And, whenever she could, Dianne went along.

"It's great having someone to ride with," she explained as they made their way across the browning pasture.

He had to agree that it was fun to have someone to ride with; especially someone like Dianne. He could ask her things he did not know, and she would give him an answer without laughing at him.

As the weeks went by Russ Masters's skill improved. He seemed to have a natural ability that increased with each passing day. Dianne was the first to see it.

"You ought to be out for the school rodeo team," she told him one afternoon when he was helping her with her goat tying.

41

"You've got to be kidding," he said. "About the only horse I've been on more than a few times has been my own. A bucking horse would throw me as high as the windmill."

"I've been thrown more times than I can remember," she told him. "It's not so bad unless you happen to land wrong."

"I'll take your word for it."

The next time they were together she handed him a rope and insisted that he see what he could do with a lariat.

He shook out the loop and spun it clumsily. "It takes more than a rope to make a roper," he muttered.

"Here, let me show you." She shook out a loop, spun it about her head and snaked it expertly over the goat Russ had been trying to rope. "It's easy."

"It doesn't look so easy to me." He tried hard, but could not drop the rope over the post he had been aiming at.

"Widen your loop," she directed, "and put a little more wrist action into spinning it."

He had been encouraged when Dianne told him that, but it was not long until he realized that there was more to it than she had indicated. It was so difficult he would have quit if it had not been for Dianne. She had such confidence in him that he could not let her down. So he kept working. After he began to master the technique, he began to enjoy roping.

As the days passed, he continued to improve. He soon graduated from roping stationary objects to those that moved. It was difficult to work with calves. They had a way of tossing their heads or darting to one side or the other at the last instant, causing the rope to miss. Nevertheless, he kept at it, moving on foot among the wiry young animals. He selected one that was within range and arched his loop toward the young steer. More often than not he missed, but by that time he was determined to learn to rope, so he kept at it tirelessly.

When he could do a passable job of roping calves on foot, he moved to horseback. That was even harder. He had to synchronize the moves of the horse and those of the calf he was trying to rope. At that point he was not pushing the calf to run. In fact, if that happened, he was undone. Finally, however, he reached a certain degree of proficiency and was ready to rope animals that were moving faster.

Russ was spending so much time at the Varner place working, riding, and roping that he neglected to practice with Chuck.

"Dad's really gettin' uptight about it," his older brother told him.

Russ felt the color rush to his cheeks. "I've had a lot of things to do," he explained lamely.

"Like what?"

The younger boy shrugged.

That night after dinner Mr. Masters called Russ into the family room and wanted to know why he had not been working out. Russ tried to explain, but his dad was not listening.

"When we bought you a horse I thought it was going to be something of a hobby," he said, sternly. "I didn't know you would let it come between you and football."

Russ hesitated. He wanted to tell his dad that the quarter horse meant more to him than doing all the things Chuck did on the gridiron—even making all-state quarterback two years in a row. Instead, he remained silent, fighting his sudden anger.

Mr. Masters leaned forward. "I know what Dusty means

to you and I'm glad you love him so much, but I don't want you to get so wrapped up in that horse that you'll regret it later. You've been around Chuck long enough to know that anybody who makes it big in football, or anything else, has to work hard at it.''

There was a brief pause before Mr. Masters cleared his throat and went on. "Let's face it. Chuck has a lot more natural ability than you have, Russ. That isn't your fault. It's just the way things happen. But you can make it big in football, too. The only difference is that you'll have to work harder.''

Russ Masters squirmed, trying to think of some way to end the conversation. He could not help it if he could not play football as well as Chuck did. He could not help it that everybody looked up to his older brother because of everything he could do. It was not Chuck's fault that he was so talented, either. They were both caught in the same vicious set of circumstances.

Mr. Masters stopped talking, and Russ got to his feet.

"How about practicing a little harder?" his dad asked. "OK?"

Russ nodded wordlessly.

"Just forget about spending all that time with your horse and put more effort into the things that count."

6

Mr. Masters and Chuck tried to talk Russ into going out for junior varsity basketball, but he convinced them it would cause his grades to suffer. Even as he spoke he knew that what he said was not quite true. His grades were at an acceptable level, and it would take more than basketball to bring them down.

Russ was somewhat ashamed of his decision not to play. He was skilled enough to make the team. There was even a good chance that he could be on the starting five. The big reason he did not want to play had nothing to do with any probable drop in his grades, the game, or the coach. The problem was his dad and Chuck. They pushed so hard that he resisted their efforts, strenuously. He was determined to be Russell Jonathan Masters—a guy people liked for himself—not for his famous brother.

That was one of the reasons he enjoyed being around Dianne and her folks. They could not care less that Chuck was his relative. Russ doubted that Mr. Varner even knew he had a brother who made headlines on the sports pages every week. Even if he had, it would not have meant anything. In horses, all that counted with their neighbor was bloodlines and conformation and performance. In men and boys, he cared only about their honesty and the way they worked. As long as Russ kept his word with Mr. Varner and did what he was told, he would continue to get along with the older man.

Dianne continued to urge him to go out for the high school rodeo team. He tried to explain why he could not, but she had difficulty understanding what he tried to tell her.

"You handle a lariat with the best of them," she said. "You'll do well in breakaway roping."

"But what about a horse for this year?" he asked, hoping he posed a difficulty she could not answer. "Dusty isn't ready and won't be for this summer."

"You can ride Shadow," she said quickly. "He's so good everybody on our roping team would ride him if I'd let them."

"But—"

She stopped currying Shadow and faced Russ, a chill creeping into her voice. "But what?" she challenged.

"That's not the whole reason," he said, miserably. "In fact, that's not the reason at all. If you have to know, I was just using it as an excuse."

She curried and brushed Shadow's withers and back before continuing. "Have you decided you don't like roping?" she persisted.

"It's not that, either," he blurted. And then, because he had no other choice, he explained why he could not consider going out for the roping team. "It's not that I don't want to," he said. "I'd rather rope or ride than anything else I know. But there's no use in even thinking about it. Dad and Chuck are insisting I go out for track this spring."

"Why?"

"According to Dad, any serious football player goes out

46

for track to keep in shape and build up his legs and his speed.''

"I've never heard anything so stupid." She faced him. "Why go out for track if you don't like it?''

He bristled slightly. "It's not as bad as all that.''

"But you said—''

"I know what I said! I'll be going out for track to help my football.''

Bewilderment clouded her eyes. "But I thought—''

"Oh, skip it! OK?''

She turned back to her horse, her temper rising, and for several minutes she curried Shadow furiously. Russ finished what he was doing and left for home, without even saying good-bye. If that was the way she felt, he told himself, testily, let her. He was not going to have her or anyone else order him around. The next day he had to go back to the Varner place to help Dianne's dad and to feed and water Dusty. He did not go near the house, however. He did not even look in that direction.

When they met in the halls at school the following week, she spoke to him curtly. He did the same, trying to match her, tone for tone. It was Saturday morning before they talked to each other again. He went over to help Mr. Varner at the usual time, thinking he would be hauling hay or working with a couple of young horses they were breaking. But his employer glanced at the sky and observed that it was going to warm up that morning.

"Get some goats in the corral," he said. "Dianne's anxious to work out with them, now that spring's about here.''

Russ stared at him uneasily. "But I thought—''

"I've got to get to town," his employer cut in. "And I don't have anything else for you to do until I get back. OK?''

Russ wanted to tell him that it was not OK. He and Dianne were scarcely speaking. He would rather be cleaning out the barn or mending fence or anything else except helping that stubborn girl. But he had to do what Mr. Varner wanted him to. There was no getting out of it. He was watering Dusty when she came striding up.

"I just want you to know that this isn't my idea," she informed him icily. "I didn't have a thing to do with it."

"Neither did I."

The muscles about her mouth tightened. "Nobody said you did."

Dusty had finished drinking by this time. Russ swung into the saddle and was about to ride off, intent on following his employer's orders.

"I'll get the goats when I'm ready," Dianne called after him.

"I'll get the goats. I don't work for you. I work for your dad."

"You leave those goats alone. I'll take care of Dad."

The corners of his mouth twitched. "I'm supposed to bring them in and help you," he repeated. "That's exactly what I'm goin' to do."

She whirled abruptly and flounced into the barn. By the time Russ reached the goats and had turned them toward the corral she was galloping their direction, her hair flying in the wind. He expected her to scatter the wiry little animals, deliberately, but she swung off to one side far enough to avoid startling them.

"I told you I don't want you around, Russ. I can manage."

For a moment he hesitated. "It'll be easier if I help." Surprisingly, even to him, much of the bite had left his voice.

48

"I can't argue with that," she replied impulsively, a smile warming her attractive young features.

Russ knew then, by the look in her eyes, that they were friends once more. Together they got the goats into the corral and closed the gate. The boy caught one of them, fastened a collar about its neck, snapped a rope into the ring, and led the strenuously protesting animal out to a post where he tethered him on a fifteen-foot length of rope. Dianne fished the stopwatch from the pocket of her jeans and handed it to him.

"As long as you're here, you'd just as well time me."

She mounted Shadow and rode him slowly to the starting gate her dad had rigged the proper distance from the post.

"Tell me when you're ready!"

She nodded, turning Shadow and standing in the stirrups. The leather tying thong was in her mouth. She raised her hand and brought it down sharply. At the same time she lowered herself into the saddle and kicked her mount in the flanks.

The powerful animal leaped into a dead run, stretching out along the ground. Nearing the goat, Dianne reined Shadow to a stop and in one smooth motion she leaped from the saddle and rushed over to the tethered billy goat. She grasped him under the flanks and lifted, pushing her knees against his body, until he went down. With one hand holding a hind leg, she whipped the thong from her mouth and lashed the goat's rear legs and one front leg securely together. It was obvious, even to a greenhorn like Russ, that Dianne had not tied a goat for some time. She fumbled with the thong and lost the front leg twice. Nevertheless, Russ called out, "Not bad!"

"How was my time?" she asked, panting heavily.

He checked the stopwatch. "Twenty-one point six seconds."

"That wouldn't even bring me twelfth place in a thirteen contestant event," she told him.

Mounting Shadow once more, she tried again. That try was a little better and the third an improvement over the second. She continued to work out an hour or more, changing goats every two or three times, to keep from wearing them out. Finally, she decided to quit for the day.

"But we've got time to bring in a few calves so you can try your hand with the rope again, Russ," she told him, squinting up at the sun to check the approximate time.

He shook his head. No matter how good he was, he would not get a chance to compete in the rodeo events. He would be out for the dashes or the high hurdles and relay.

Mr. Varner came up in his pickup just then, and Russ helped him unload the sacked oats he had bought in town. The Masters boy was glad to have a chance to get away from Dianne. She could not bug him about doing what he wanted to with his life, if he was not there.

At church the next morning the pastor repeated an announcement for the youth retreat the following weekend. It was being held in the Bible camp fifteen miles or so east of town, and reservations had to be in the youth pastor's hands by Wednesday afternoon.

"You can leave your reservations with the church office, Pastor Stovall, or Chuck Masters," the senior minister concluded.

Russ squirmed. He had forgotten all about the retreat, but he knew he would be expected to go, whether he wanted to or not. Chuck had probably put his name on the list already and picked up the reservations fee from their dad. Right now he was stuck with that kind of stuff, he told himself, but the time would come when he would be able to do as he pleased. Then they would find out that he had a mind of his own.

Russ had not even thought that Dianne might be interested in going until his mother mentioned it on the way home from church.

"I was talking to Mrs. Varner a few days ago," she said, "and she told me she'd like to have Dianne take in the retreat."

"I didn't know you were acquainted with Mrs. Varner," Russ said, curious.

"I wasn't until you started going over there. Then I went to see her, and we became real good friends. We've even started having a Bible study together."

That surprised Russ even more than the fact that his mother and Pamela Varner were friends. As far as he knew, the Varners never went to church. For that matter he could not remember having seen a Bible around the house.

"When you go over to Varners' tomorrow, will you take a registration blank for her to sign and pick up the fee?"

"I—I guess so," he said without enthusiasm.

Chuck's smile widened. "It isn't everybody who'll have his girl friend there."

"Hang it on your ear!" Russ grumbled.

"Sandy'll be there," Chuck said. "I think it's great that you'll have Dianne there, too."

"Knock it off, OK? I don't have to do *everything* you do!"

The silence hung between them.

The next afternoon Russ burst into his room after school,

changed clothes hurriedly, and was at the door on the way to the Varner ranch when his mother reminded him about the form he was to take to Dianne. He had forgotten that Dianne had a dental appointment that afternoon and did not remember it until he was rapping on the back door. From somewhere inside the German shepherd barked.

"Duke!" he called loudly. By this time the dog knew his voice and accepted him as a friend. The instant Duke heard who was there he fell silent.

"Come on in, Russ!" Mrs. Varner exclaimed. "The door's unlocked."

He opened it and stepped into the bright, cheery kitchen. The table was set for two, which told Russ that Grant Varner was away again, and the delightful aroma of chili filled the room. Russ was about to call out to Dianne's mother when he heard the muffled sound of her wheelchair, and she appeared in the dining room doorway.

"I was sure it was you," she said.

There was a disturbing tone in her voice—a sadness he had never heard before.

"Is there something wrong?" he asked.

"What could possibly be wrong on such a beautiful spring day?"

"I—I just thought something was bothering you."

For a moment tears glistened in her eyes and her lips quavered. Then a smile broke through. "I'm feeling fine, Russ," she managed. "Just fine."

He hesitated, staring at her. He had no reason for believing that she was not telling the truth, but he still felt uneasy. Until now she had always been so jolly he had been amazed at her. This time, however, she was different. She seemed to be trying hard to make him believe she was the same as ever, but he was sure it was only an act.

He sat down at the kitchen table and visited with her for a few minutes before giving her the reservation form for Dianne.

"I'll have it ready for you tomorrow." Her smile widened again, so happily that he began to wonder if he had erred in thinking that she was disturbed. He was at the door when she stopped him.

"And Russ," she began, "there is a favor I'd like to ask of you."

"Sure thing." He turned back.

"I don't know whether Mr. Varner will be home before the retreat or not, but if he is, please don't say anything to him about this, will you?"

"Not if you don't want me to," he replied.

"I think it would be best if we keep this our little secret," she answered, her voice faltering. "You see, Grant doesn't understand about such things."

7

Russ was not quite sure he wanted to go to the youth retreat. The last time had been a terrible drag. He did not even want to think about going again. At least that was the way he tried to make himself believe he felt about camp. The truth was, however, that he had a nagging suspicion in the inner reaches of his heart that there was more to his reluctance than that.

The last time he was there he had been under such deep conviction he could not sleep. He turned and tossed miserably, and when he finally fell asleep the first gray fingers of the false dawn reached over the horizon. He did not want to go through that again, but he knew it was best if he did not resist his parents and Chuck. They had ways of putting pressure on that really bugged him.

Besides, Dianne was going to be there.

If Chuck or any of the other guys had insisted that he was going because he enjoyed her company, there would have been a fierce argument. He could not admit that, even to himself. He still flushed when Chuck or his dad teased him about spending more time than necessary at the Varner place. Still, he had to admit that she might have a little something to do with his willingness to go this time.

Russ had not expected Dianne to question him about what went on during the weekend at Bible camp. Such activities had become such a regular part of his life he assumed everyone knew what a retreat was like. When they were feeding her dad's horses in the corral, however, she voiced her misgivings.

"Mom's all excited about this retreat business your church is having at Cedar Lake," she said. "What is it all about?"

He eyed her narrowly. "It's just a youth retreat."

She stopped what she was doing and faced him. "And what's that?"

He glanced helplessly at her.

"What's it like?" she persisted.

"It's a lot of fun," he said, wondering why he was giving her such a glowing report of something he felt was such a bummer. "We'll play games in the afternoon when we get there, and have a great meal. When that's over some guys and gals'll get out their guitars and have some stunts and gags around the campfire. Then, about nine o'clock or so we'll goof around for about an hour before going to bed. It's a blast."

"There's got to be more than that to it," she answered, suspiciously. "What's the catch?"

He cut the twine on another bale and forked the alfalfa into the mangers that stretched along the far end of the long row of stalls. Dianne began to measure out the oats in the feed boxes, a can full for each horse. He waited until she had finished.

"What do you think it's like?"

"Well—" She stopped what she was doing and leaned against the rough board partition. "I figure they'll hammer at us to get us saved or born again or whatever it is you call it." She paused significantly. "Am I right or am I right?"

"There'll probably be some preaching," he admitted. Although he had attacked the camp for the same reasons at home, it disturbed him to hear Dianne say the same things. He felt as though he had to defend the church and youth leaders. "They may share Christ with us," he answered lamely, "and give us a chance to confess our sin and—and put our trust in Christ—but there won't be any pressure put on anybody. That I can guarantee."

"I'll bet!"

"It's the truth."

"Sure," she countered. "Sure, it's the truth. I believe you."

He caught the sarcasm in her voice and turned away in an effort to end the conversation before he said something to make her angry again. Still, she refused to stop.

"It's like Dad says. All the church really cares about is getting all the money it can out of people and controlling their lives. They don't want us to have any fun."

"There might be churches like that," he answered, his voice rising, "but ours isn't that way. Our minister preaches that God loves us and wants to save us so we'll go to heaven and be with Him."

She came around to where he was standing. "That's what you say, but look at my mother! She's in a wheelchair and will be for the rest of her life. If God loves her so much, why would He allow a terrible thing like that to happen?"

"I don't know why He let your mother be in a wheel-chair," Russ answered, "but I do know that God loves us."

"You'll never make me buy that!" she cried, her eyes blazing. "I believe the same as my Dad. If there is a God and He would let a terrible thing like Mom's injury happen to such a wonderful person, I don't want to have anything to do with Him.''

After that outburst Russ was sure Dianne would not be going to the retreat, but he was wrong. When the kids gathered at the church after school Dianne was there with her sleeping bag and a small overnight case.

"So you decided to come after all," he exclaimed.

"It wasn't my idea. Mom felt so bad when I told her I wasn't going that I changed my mind."

A couple of her girl friends came up just then and asked her to be in their cabin. Moments later they piled into the back seat of the station wagon and were on their way to the camp. Russ turned and went back to where Chuck and Larry Goddard were standing beside his brother's old car.

"Oh, are you going to ride with us?" Chuck asked, winking at his pal. "I thought you'd be riding with your girl friend."

Russ knew his face was scarlet. "Lay off, will you?"

At Bible camp an hour or so later Russ saw Dianne at a distance. He wanted to go over and talk to her, but she was with some other girls, and he could not bring himself to brave their snickers and knowing glances. Again at dinner he tried to get close enough to talk to her, but her friends were still clustered around her. It was not until the campers gathered at the lake for the campfire service that he was able to approach her.

"Having fun?"

"Until now," she retorted, the muscles in her lower jaw tightening.

"Because I came around?" he asked.

"You know that's not the reason."

A moment later the guitarist struck a chord to bring them to attention. Slowly the conversation halted. Russ turned toward the fire. He did not know why, but he always enjoyed those meetings at night.

The wind had dropped to a whisper, but the early spring chill was still drifting off the lake. The kids moved closer together and closer to the fire. They sang a few songs, and the leader asked for testimonies. As Russ knew he would be, Chuck was among the first to get to his feet. He told them how he had been drawn to God as a kid in Sunday school, but had resisted yielding his heart and his life to Christ until he had come out to this very same spot to a campfire service as a seventh grader.

"That night," he said seriously, "I realized that I—Chuck Masters—had to make a decision regarding Jesus Christ. I had to face up to the fact that I was a sinner headed for an eternity in hell unless I confessed my sin and put my faith in Christ."

More than once Russ had told his friends, scornfully, that he had heard Chuck give his testimony so often he could give it, himself. This time, however, it was different. God seemed to be using the words to challenge him in a way that he had never been challenged before. He was still thinking about what his brother had said when the meeting drew to a close and the invitation had been given.

He glanced at Dianne, who was standing, ramrod straight, beside him. It was all he could do to keep from holding up his hand, or pushing forward to the place where the youth pastor was standing.

Had it not been for Dianne, he would not have been able to resist the insistent tugging at his heart. Or, if she had shown some indication of softening, he could not have refrained from taking a stand for Christ. But he knew what she was thinking. Her jaw was set, and her eyes were stonehard. And, while Russ battled with himself, the meeting ended and the opportunity was gone.

For a moment he remained motionless. Strangely, at least to him—Dianne remained beside him.

"Well," he said, lamely, "what did you think of it?"

"I thought I would freeze to death," she retorted, shivering.

Disappointment clouded his young features. "I'm sorry you're so cold," he told her. "I thought we could go to the snack shop for some ice cream. We don't have to be in our cabins for another hour."

"That sounds like a good idea," she said, quickly.

"But I—"

Her laughter trilled. "I'd rather be cold than go back to our cabin and sit in on the prayer meeting they're planning. A prayer meeting! That's the pits!"

Her words drove a spear into his heart.

They left the dying embers of the campfire and sauntered toward the snack shop.

"I was surprised to hear Chuck talk the way he did," she began. "He sounded like a preacher about a hundred years old."

Russ nodded.

"I can't understand why anyone with so much on the ball would be like that," she continued, turning to stare at the broad expanse of water. For a moment she remained silent, studying the black surface of the lake and the star-dotted sky. "Why would he want to throw his life away?"

"What do you mean?"

"All that talk about giving Christ control.—Look at the

things he can do. He's great at just about anything he tries.''

"What's that got to do with following Christ?"

She hesitated. "I don't know, but he's got so much going for him I wouldn't think he would need religion.''

"He doesn't feel that way."

Her smile pleaded with him to change the subject to safer ground, and he allowed her to do so. She talked brightly as they got their ice cream and found a place apart from the others, where they sat down together.

Russ made remarks at times that he hoped were appropriate, but in truth, he scarcely heard her. His own heart was churning, and thoughts raced like stampeding cattle through his mind. He was lost. If something happened to him that night, he would not go to heaven. The realization was staggering. Nervously he wiped a hand across his forehead.

"Russ, is there something wrong? You look as though you don't feel good.''

"I've got a little headache," he lied. "That's all."

"I hope I didn't cause it by telling you what I think of your brother's religion.''

"No way. I think it's weird, myself."

She got quickly to her feet. "Let's forget about Chuck. OK?''

"Yeah."

A few minutes before ten o'clock, when they were all to be inside, he took her to her cabin.

"I'm glad I came," she said softly, her hand resting on his for a moment. "It has been fun."

He waited until the door closed behind her. Then he made his way down the path to his own cabin. Why had he lied to Dianne? He had always taken satisfaction in the fact that he told the truth, regardless of the consequences. A knife

60

turned deep in his stomach, and he winced at the pain. He was no different than the guys who did not know Christ as their Savior.

His counselor met him just outside the door.

"I was just going to look for you, Russ," he said, sternly. "It's after ten."

"Not very much."

"You know the rules."

"It took a little longer to walk back from Dianne's cabin than I figured." There! He had lied again. The truth was that he had been in such turmoil he stopped in the path, trying to sort out his tangled thoughts. He did not know how long he had been there, but it must have been far longer than he had supposed.

"I'll have to report this to Pastor Stovall tomorrow morning."

Russ glared at him. "You do that."

8

Russ Masters pushed rudely by the counselor and stormed inside, unmindful of the fact that the lights were out and everyone else was in bed. He stumbled over a chair and lunged against the bunk on the opposite wall.

"Hey, watch it, Masters!" the occupant of the top bunk exclaimed.

"Yeh," somebody else cried. "Watch it, Masters."

The cry went up and for a moment everyone in the cabin was yelling at him.

"Pipe down, will you?" Right then he did not feel like taking part in their fun and games. He made his way to his own bunk and shucked his shoes.

"It sure took you a long time to kiss her good night!" one of the guys put in.

"Maybe she couldn't bear to have him leave her!"

"Cool it!" Russ sputtered.

By this time the counselor was back inside. "All right, you guys! Lights out means mouths shut. OK?"

"We were just finding out what took Russ so long."

He got into his pajamas and crawled into bed, grateful for the darkness that hid the scarlet in his cheeks.

He lay motionless on the hard mattress, staring up at the springs of the bed above him. There would be little reason for Stovall to crack down on him. The retreat would be over shortly after lunch and everybody would be going home. There was not much that could happen to him at camp.

He should have been relieved at that, but he was not. His dad had a thing about obeying counselors and keeping camp regulations. Russ figured he might be grounded for a week or so or be forbidden to ride Dusty. Either punishment would be harder on him than anything the camp director would mete out.

He hoped, however, that he could keep Dianne from learning the reason for any such problems he might have. She could get the idea that it was her fault, and it really was not. He had been late getting back to his cabin because his heart and mind were churning so furiously he lost all sense of time. Even now the things Chuck had said were of far more concern than any punishment that might come his way.

The wages of sin is death, a Bible verse shouted at him from the inner reaches of his mind, *but the gift of God is eternal life through Jesus Christ our Lord.*

He had tried to make himself believe he lived such a good life he would not need saving in order to get to heaven, but that verse ripped away the deception he had woven around himself. If he had not known it before, he would have realized it that night. He had lied to Dianne, and later he had lied to his counselor. That sort of thing had never before struck him as being dishonest. It probably would not have bothered him then if it had not been for Chuck's testimony and the Bible verses that pushed their barbs into his own consciousness.

Russ raised himself on one elbow and stared into the darkness of the cabin. The muscles in his throat tightened, and he clenched his fist, gripping the outer edge of his sleeping bag until his fingers ached. He did not care how miserable he was, he told himself, grimly. He was not stupid enough to make a fool of himself over religion.

He twisted and tossed restlessly until morning wakened the other guys and he could get up.

"I thought you'd be in bed, dreaming," Steve Blair said from his bunk across the cabin.

"About sweet Dianne," someone else added.

"Stow it!" he grumbled.

"Maybe she gave him the old heave-ho last night!"

"See that dreamy look in his eyes? Nothing like that happened."

"Bug off! All of you!"

But they did not stop. They were still taunting him when they went to the dining hall for breakfast.

He looked warily for her so he could sit at a table as far from her as possible. It was not that he wanted to avoid her. He just had to get the guys off his back, some way. She was there when he came in, standing in line some distance ahead of him. She glanced his direction and waved discreetly. He returned the wave, hoping his friends had not seen him.

If they had, the sudden appearance of the youth pastor kept them from saying anything. Pastor Stovall stepped into the long building, eyes searching the line of campers for his target. Russ knew who he was looking for and cringed, suddenly afraid that Dianne would see what was happening and think that she was responsible. Then he remembered this was the first time she had been to camp so she would not know the regulations.

"I'd like to have you come over to the camp office when you finish breakfast, Russ," the minister said, quietly. "OK?"

As far as Russ was concerned he would rather have gone to the office immediately and learned what was going to happen to him, but there was no chance of that. He would have to wait.

Pastor Stovall was waiting for him when he went to the office later. He wanted to know the reason for Russ's being out after ten o'clock the night before.

The boy shrugged.

"Don't you have anything to say?" the youth minister asked. "Any explanation?"

He shook his head.

"Frankly, I was surprised when your name was on the report this morning. I'm even more surprised that you refuse to give me a reason for your being late. We've never had a problem with Chuck."

"But I'm not Chuck!" Russ retorted curtly.

"It might be wise if you followed his example."

Although turmoil churned in his heart Russ remained silent while he was being lectured. The conversation ended a few minutes later with Russ's being confined to his cabin during the recreation period. He left almost gratefully. At least he would not have to face the guys from his cabin for a bit longer. They had been with him when he was summoned to the office. Sooner or later he would have to explain, but he might feel more like it after a while.

Russ crossed the grounds hurriedly and went inside, closing the door behind him. He threw himself on his bunk and lay there for several minutes, staring up at the link springs and the mattress on the bunk above. Before long everybody in church would know what he had done. And the story would grow as it spread.

But that was not the worst of it. He could hear the older

people now. "He's certainly not the boy Chuck is!"

He swung his feet over the side of the bed and sat up. He knew *why* he was different than his older brother, aside from the fact that Chuck was bigger and smarter and more athletic and better liked. Russ was not a believer. All of his going to Sunday school and church and youth group was a sham. His praying in public and giving his testimony did not mean a thing, either. He had learned the right words and the right time to say them, but his heart was untouched.

Russ paced noisily to the window and looked out. Dianne was on one team in a game they were playing. She was standing a bit to one side, looking around. And he knew why. She was wondering what had happened to him. That meant he would have to explain to her, too. He moved angrily from the window, trying to figure out what he could tell her that would not make her think he was a dope. Moments later he picked up his Bible and fingered it pensively, as though undecided about reading it. Then he slammed it into his suitcase and closed the top.

He did not know for sure what he would tell Dianne when she asked him why he was not on one team or the other, but he could not tell her that he was being treated like a little kid who got caught with his hand in the cookie jar. He was too proud for that.

Whatever he told her would be a lie. *But what difference would that make?* he asked himself. His entire life was a lie.

He tried to keep out of her way without making it too obvious, but he could not avoid her at lunch. He was standing in line to pick up his food when she came in and stood beside him. Just as he expected, she wanted to know where he had been.

"Those games get so boring I duck out every chance I get," he exclaimed, looking away so she could not read the truth in his eyes.

She studied him curiously. "I thought it was sort of fun."

"Sometimes it's not so bad," he acknowledged, "but today wasn't one of those times." He did not know whether that explanation satisfied her or not, but it must have. She changed the subject.

Russ was afraid his older brother would tell their folks what had happened at camp, but he did not even say anything about it to Russ. That, more than anything, made Russ wonder whether he even knew.

That afternoon as soon as they got back from camp Russ went over to take care of Dusty. Mr. Varner was there, poking around the barn, a nasty frown darkening his ruddy face.

"And where've you been?" he demanded, irritably.

Russ winced under his cold stare. "At Cedar Lake," he replied, defensively. "I talked with you about it last week."

That seemed to stop Mr. Varner. He straightened slowly. "Are you the one who got Dianne to go out there?"

The boy hesitated. He had not had anything to do with it, and that was the truth.

"Did *you* get Dianne to go to that Bible camp?"

The boy hesitated. He had not had much to do with it, but he did not know whether he could convince Mr. Varner of that, or not.

"No way," he retorted firmly. "I didn't even know about her going until—"

"Until what?"

A sudden loyalty swept over Russ. He wanted to protect his mother by admitting responsibility, but Dianne's dad had warned him about lying to him, and she had also told him of the importance of always telling her dad the truth. Russ was afraid he would be in big trouble if he lied.

"I—"

"Until what?" Varner repeated. "You were going to say you didn't know anything about Dianne going to Bible camp until that mother of yours talked my wife into signing for Dianne." He sounded as though his daughter had been lured to some terrible, evil place. "Is that it?"

"I—I did tell Dianne that the camp is a real neat place to go." He felt obligated to defend his mother as much as possible. "You can't blame it on Mom," he answered. "I—I'm responsible, too."

"I don't blame it on your mother!" Mr. Varner exclaimed, his eyes narrowing. "And I don't blame it on you! It's Pam's fault!" Anger etched his harsh voice. "She knows how I feel about religion! She had no cause to go against me!"

He picked up his pitchfork and threw it halfway across the barn. The tines drove into the rough pine planking so savagely that they quivered like so many tuning forks. "And you, Masters!" His lips curled bitterly, and a violent curse startled the boy. "You'd better find another place to keep your horse. I don't want you around here anymore!"

Russ Masters stared helplessly at him. "But—"

"You've got till a week from next Monday. If you haven't got him out of here by then I'm goin' to turn him loose. Y'understand?"

He nodded, crushed by the sudden development.

"I don't want you hangin' around Dianne or Pam," he informed Russ evenly. "And you can tell that mother of yours that she's not welcome anymore. The Bible study, or whatever they call it, is going to stop!"

Mechanically Russ took care of Dusty and left the yard, mindful of the fact that Dianne was standing at the kitchen window. Why had he not told Mr. Varner he was just like him—that he did not buy that Christian bit, either?

He wondered if it would do any good to go back and try to tell him? Or would he think Russ was just talking that way so he could keep Dusty at the Varner place and go on working there? It would not do any good, he decided, at last. He knew Mr. Varner was too mad to listen to him.

At home a few minutes later his folks saw the clouds in his eyes and wanted to know what was wrong.

"I've got to find a new place to keep Dusty."

"I'm not surprised," Mrs. Masters said. "Pam phoned this morning and told me that she wouldn't be able to study the Bible with me any more."

"I don't see why he had to blame me for it," Russ complained. "I didn't have a thing to do with that—or getting Dianne to go out to camp, either."

"Would you like to have Dad phone and tell him that?" his mother asked.

"He wouldn't listen."

She went over and put an arm about his shoulder. "I'm sorry I have caused you so much trouble, Russ," she said, "but Pamela Varner is so lonely and so hungry for the Word of God—she told me she had been waiting for years for someone to come and explain salvation to her."

"She's always acted OK with me," Russ put in. "Dianne says she's never seen her unhappy."

"That's what she wants Dianne and her husband to believe, but she has times of deep depression. She said she didn't know what it was to be truly happy until she confessed her sin and put her trust in Jesus Christ for salvation.''

Russ scowled. His mother had caused the trouble, and he had to pay the price for it.

He did not even like to think about eating dinner that night, but he knew there would only be a hassle if he stayed in his room, so he joined the rest of the family in the big kitchen. His dad told him he would start work on the stable right away. That helped some, but he still had been robbed of an opportunity to work with Mr. Varner and learn from him. Someone else caused the trouble, but he had to pay the price.

Monday morning Dianne talked to Russ in the hall at school. She was sorry her father had been so angry and unreasonable with him and insisted that he find another place to keep his horse.

"The worst of it is," he said, "I didn't have anything to do with your going to that retreat."

"That's what Mother and I told him," she said. "But he wouldn't pay any attention to us."

He managed a thin smile. "Thanks, Dianne."

That afternoon he went out to see if he could find someone who was willing to take Dusty in. The first place he stopped was already boarding two horses. They did not have either the space or the hay for another animal. The next man was running a small herd of cattle and was afraid a horse among them would not be wise.

Russ only understood that the man did not want Dusty on his place. Tears smarted in his eyes as he noted the position of the sun on the horizon and turned to peddle back to Varners' to feed and water his horse. Mr. Varner was in the yard working on the pickup as he arrived, but acted as though he had not even seen him.

Monday was a foreshadow of the rest of the week. Russ went to everyone he could think of in an effort to find someone to keep his horse. The reasons were different, but the answers were the same. Nobody was willing to provide space for him. Russ talked the problem over with his dad.

"I called a couple of contractors earlier in the week, Russ," he said. "The best I can do is to have the stable started in a couple of weeks."

"A couple of weeks?" he echoed. "I've got to have him away from Mr. Varner's by next Monday."

Russ kept on trying to find a place for Dusty until his dad got the stable built, but it was useless. Everyone who wanted to board horses already had all he could handle. Or so it seemed.

On Thursday night Chuck asked him to go out to the Bible camp to help paint some of the buildings to get things ready for the summer camping season, but he refused. Finding a place for Dusty was his excuse.

Chuck and his pals left Platte Valley at seven o'clock Saturday morning. The back of his old car was filled with paint and brushes and old clothes. Russ listened to their laughter and for a moment wished he were going along. It sounded as though they were going to have a great time.

Russ left the house a short time after his brother and his friends had climbed into the old car and driven away. He spent most of the day searching the area for someone who would take in Dusty for a couple of weeks. Shortly after six that evening he quit trying to find a temporary home for his horse and headed back to his dad's place, no nearer a solution than before.

71

When eight o'clock came and Chuck had not yet come home, his parents were concerned and asked Russ if he had seen his older brother. "Nope." If he was the one who was missing, he decided, they would assume he was goofing off somewhere, but not good, old dependable Chuck. He was seldom late for a meal.

"There's a Campus Life meeting tonight," Mr. Masters said, trying to hide his uneasiness. "The boys might have worked later than they planned and decided to go straight to the meeting."

Time dragged slowly by. In a way Russ was glad it was happening. Maybe it would show them that his older brother was not as perfect as they always thought he was. At 9:30 Larry Goddard's mother phoned to see if Mr. and Mrs. Masters had heard from the boys. When she hung up, Mrs. Ketler called to see if Dennis was there.

The clock was striking 10:00 when a car pulled into the driveway.

"There Chuck is now," Mrs. Masters said, relief evident in her voice.

But there was a knock at the door, and her husband went to answer it. A highway patrolman was standing on the porch, nervously.

"Mr. Masters," he began, "I'm afraid I have some very bad news for you. Your son has been in an accident!"

9

Russ was in the family room watching the sports report on the local TV station when the patrolman came to the house. He heard the doorbell ring and was aware that someone was talking to his dad, but that was all. It was not the sort of thing to cause alarm. His mother often said their house was like O'Hare Airport in Chicago or the Nebraska stadium the day of a Big Red game, so many were constantly coming and going. For that reason Russ thought nothing of it. Moments later, as the front door closed, a news bulletin flashed on the screen.

"One Platte Valley student was killed and two injured—one seriously—in a two-car accident early this evening on the old Oregon Highway fourteen miles east of town. Names are being withheld pending notification of the next of kin. We will bring you more details of the accident at the conclusion of this program."

Russ's throat tightened convulsively—and, for a terrible instant, fear squeezed the breath from his lungs. He stood mechanically and started for the living room. His parents met him in the doorway. The instant he saw his dad's ashen face and the tears in his mother's eyes he knew what had happened.

73

"Chuck?" he asked, the name choking in his larynx.

Mr. Masters nodded almost imperceptibly. "He was killed in an accident on the viaduct just out of Fairfield." His voice was hollow and expressionless, completely devoid of emotion, as though something within him had died with the officer's knock on the door.

Russ recoiled at the news. It did not seem real, somehow. This was only an ugly dream, a bitter charade that would soon be over, leaving him weak and shaken.

"What happened?" he asked.

"A car without lights veered across the road as they came off the viaduct and hit them head on," he continued. "I doubt that Chuck even saw it before it slammed into him."

His mother went to Russ and enveloped him in her arms. She clung to him, her tears dampening his cheek. Russ did not cry. He could not. His chest was caught in a savage, vicelike grip that forced him to fight for breath. He remained motionless, staring straight ahead and listening to the TV announcer. He could not speak, or even think.

The cultured voice from the local television station turned rough and brutish as it violated the sprawling house. Finally he could stand it no longer. He pushed his mother away and strode to the console where he switched off the TV. The silence was deafening and he reached down, impulsively, to turn it on again. He had his hand on the knob when his dad ordered him to leave it alone.

"Nobody feels like watching that thing!" he snarled.

Russ winced as though he had been slapped and turned quickly away to hide the hurt in his eyes. Now that he thought about it, he realized how shocking it was to his parents for him to even think of turning television on. Did it mean that he did not care that his brother was gone?

74

A terrible revulsion swept over him. What kind of a guy would his folks think he was after doing a stupid thing like that? He expelled his breath with a rush. He did not know what was wrong with him. Now his mom and dad probably thought he did not care that Chuck had been killed.

And he did! The pain in his young frame was almost unbearable.

Mechanically the lithe fourteen-year-old moved to the broad family room window and stared out into the blackness of the night. Although he did not turn to see, he was certain that his dad must be staring at him with as much disgust as he felt for himself. All he could hear was his mother's hushed weeping. He wanted to throw his arms about them and tell them how sorry he was about Chuck and that he hurt so much he scarcely knew what he was doing.

He yearned for the feel of his mother's arms around him to help ease the torment that churned in his bewildered heart. He longed, desperately, to be young enough so he could crawl up on her lap and sob out his agony against her breast! If only his dad or mom would tell him that they *knew* he was suffering, too! Even that would help. But they did not. They were so deep in their own agony they locked him out. It was almost as though he was not a part of the family anymore.

They were probably wishing that he had been the one who had been killed instead of Chuck! Guilt and self-pity and grief slammed into him.

Russ retreated a step or two, as stiff and unfeeling as a robot. The images in the window blurred as he moved backward, and he caught the reflections of his parents in the flawless glass. Surprisingly, his dad was not looking his way at all. His eyes were fixed and staring and there was a stern set to his square-hewn jaw. Russ's mother was still sobbing—more quietly now, as though she had no wish to share her agony with anyone.

Russ was still standing at the window when Pastor Orman came to the house to talk with the family and have a time of prayer. There were certain details that had to be taken care of, he said. The reporters would be descending on the house early the next morning, if not that night, and someone would have to talk to them. The mortician had to be notified, and their relatives should be called.

"I'll take care of those details, Roger," he said quietly. "And my wife will be over as soon as she can get a few things together. She'll do the cooking and anything else that's needed until some of your family get here to take over."

Mr. and Mrs. Masters thanked him. Russ was glad the pastor had come over, too. It seemed to him that they all quieted after that. Pastor Orman's presence even had a stabilizing effect on him. The pain was still in his heart, but the calm and ordered manner of the man of God helped him as much as his parents.

"What about the other boys?" Mrs. Masters asked.

"Larry has a broken pelvis and some cracked ribs. Dennis was shaken up and cut about the face, but they don't think either of them are critically hurt."

"Did you hear exactly how the accident happened?" Russ's dad asked.

Pastor Orman nodded. "I talked to the officers who investigated. They said the boys had left the camp shortly after dark and headed toward town at a reasonable rate of speed. The driver coming from town was driving so fast and reckless there had been at least three calls to the state patrol

76

about him before the accident. Two troopers were on their way to pick him up at the time of the collision.''

The minister paused momentarily, and the corners of Roger Masters's mouth tightened. His fists clenched until the cords stood out on the backs of his hands. "The man was drunk, wasn't he?''

"They didn't say, but that seems quite evident. He was on the wrong side of the road for no reason and hit the boys head-on. He didn't have his lights on. Apparently they didn't see him until an instant before the cars hit.''

Mrs. Masters took a deep breath. "Was he hurt?'' she asked.

"Shaken up and bruised some, according to what I was told. They took him to the hospital for examination, but he was released after emergency treatment.''

"I'm glad,'' she murmured quietly.

Glad? Russ's temper flared. How could she be glad about a thing like that? The accident was all his fault. It would have served him right if he had been killed, too. That was what he deserved. If he had lost his life and Chuck and his companions had been spared it would not have been so bad. He would have brought it on himself. But Chuck had not done anything wrong. He had been going within the speed limit. Clouds covered the moon and the stars, making it darker than usual, but there had not been any rain to make the roads slick. If the other driver had been sober he would have had his lights on and would have been driving halfway decently and legally. There would not have been an accident, and Chuck would still be alive.

Why had God allowed such an awful thing to happen? And to someone who loved Him as much as Chuck had. There probably was not another guy in all of PV High who was even half as interested in the things of Christ as Chuck, or who was a better witness.

Briefly Russ's temper surged. If that was what it meant to be a Christian, he did not want anything to do with it, he told himself. Then he realized that his brother would not have liked that. When things went sour, Chuck usually voiced a quotation their mother often used. "God didn't promise us an easy life if we follow Him. He just promises to help us over the rough places."

Russ fought against his own sudden bitterness directed at a God who would allow his brother to be snatched from them. He himself was not a believer. He did not claim to be, except when some zealous Christian started pestering him. But never before had he been angry with God. Now only the firm, sure faith of his parents and his brother who was gone kept him from it. He wanted to shout to the world that he hated God, but of course he could not do that now. That would only add to his mother and dad's agony.

Those thoughts were churning through his mind when she asked him if he should not be going to bed. "You look so tired."

He hesitated, studying her gray, haggard features. "Are you and Dad going to bed now?" he asked, uneasily.

"Not for a while."

"Then I think I'll stay up, too."

His dad turned toward him as though becoming aware, for the first time, that he was still in the room. "You heard your mother! Go to bed!" he ordered sternly.

"But—" The words choked off under the stern glare of his father. Somehow he thought that by staying up he could show them how much he, too, was grieving, but there was no use in trying to voice his feelings. How could he when

78

they were vague and indistinct, only half formed in his heart?

"Go to bed, Russ!" Mr. Masters snapped, giving vent to his own bewilderment and pain. "Don't let me have to tell you again!"

"OK!" The boy jumped quickly to his feet and stormed toward his bedroom, which had been next to Chuck's. "OK!"

For an instant anger churned wildly within him—anger and that desperate loneliness that had seized him when he first learned of the accident.

Did his folks not know that his heart was also bleeding? That he could have drawn strength and help just from being with them? He did not know how he could go into his room and shut the door on the outside world, leaving him alone, empty and aching.

At Chuck's door he paused, as he often had in the past, to listen for the sound of his older brother's stereo. His parents had never known how many times he had slipped in to see his older brother when they had sent him off to bed, stopping to talk briefly.

He would never be able to do that again. Chuck was gone. Gone! He would never hear Chuck's answer to his furtive knock and dart in to talk with Chuck before going off to bed.

It can't be! he once more told himself. There had to be some mistake! Chuck was not dead! Not his brother, who had been so vibrantly alive only hours before and who had been too good to die.

Impulsively Russ opened Chuck's bedroom door and sneaked inside. His mother found him there an hour later, sprawled on the bed asleep. His tears had soaked a little spot on the spread.

The next two days dragged endlessly for Russ. It was the first time he had experienced a death in the family, and he was bewildered by the way life changed. He could never remember his dad staying home from work when he was not ill or going to a football game. He was surprised, too, at the way family and friends crowded into the house.

Aunts and uncles and cousins Russ had not seen in years came to see them. There was crying and talking and more laughter than he thought was fitting. It made him want to grab some of the loudest by the collar and ask them if they did not know that Chuck had been killed.

The presence of family and friends seemed to make Chuck's death a bit easier for his parents—particularly his mother. The color crept back into her face and she seemed to relax slightly. Yet, there were times when she was overwhelmed by the tragedy that had befallen them. An incredible sadness glazed her eyes, and the lines in her face deepened until she looked older than Grandma Wexler who hobbled painfully into church every Sunday.

Russ was so confused by what was going on that he forgot about everything else. He did not even think about his horse or the fact that he could not keep Dusty at the Varner farm any more.

Although time dragged past on feet of stone, the hour for the funeral finally arrived. At first it was to be held in the church, but when the pastor learned that school would be dismissed so the kids could attend he realized that nothing smaller than the high school gym would be large enough. By the time the crowd had filed in, every chair was filled and there were two rows of latecomers standing in the rear beneath the basketball goal.

Russ had been dreading that moment—steeling himself

against it as though it was something to be endured. He entered the gym stiffly behind his parents and took a chair on the front row. Dianne, who was sitting to one side in the bleachers, waved cautiously to him, a slight, almost imperceptible, friendly motion that was meant to tell him that she was thinking of him. He did not wave back, but was surprised at the comfort the little wave brought to him—almost like the handclasp of some of his dad's Christian friends. They were saying without words that they knew how deeply he was hurting, and they cared. He was sure that Dianne was telling him she cared, too.

A woman from the church got up to sing. He knew her well, but at the moment it was as if she was a stranger. Even the song was new to him, though he had heard it dozens of times before.

"It seems fitting, somehow," Pastor Orman began when it was time for the brief message, "to have Chuck Masters's funeral here in the gym he loved so much. He used to tell me that some of his greatest enjoyment came when he was on this court, matching wits and skill with the other teams in the Western Conference.

"Chuck was not one to push that driving desire-to-win concern to the back of his mind, nor his concern for the spiritual welfare of his friends and teammates. He not only knew and loved the Lord Jesus Christ, he actively shared his faith with those he came in contact with."

Russ sank his teeth into his lower lip as the minister spoke about Chuck's faith. For several years Russ had been able to deceive his older brother into believing that he, too, was a Christian. The last few months, however, Chuck had been getting wise to him. More often than not, when they were together, he turned the conversation to spiritual things that deeply disturbed Russ and left him shaken and so tormented he had difficulty sleeping at night.

When the message was finally over the minister said he was going to do something he had never before done at a funeral. He asked if there were those in the gymnasium who wanted to follow Chuck's example by confessing their sin and putting their trust in Christ. Almost immediately half a dozen or more did so. The homecoming queen was the first to get to her feet, followed by the offensive center who had worked so closely with Chuck on the football field. Several kids from church were among the group, and so were two of Chuck's teachers. Mrs. Masters looked around and began to cry once more, silently.

Russ's lithe young frame stiffened. For some reason Dusty came to mind. Deliberately he forced himself to think about his young quarter horse, trying to figure out where he could keep him now that Mr. Varner did not want him around their place and Russ's dad had not yet finished the stable.

When the ceremony at the cemetery was over and the family had gathered at the church for a lunch nobody really wanted, Russ slipped out and caught a ride back to the house with a friend who was going that way. He would not be missed in all that crowd, he reasoned.

At home he went into his room, changed into his jeans and denim shirt and hurried to get Dusty. The closer he got to the Varner buildings the more his pulse quickened. The deadline he had been given for moving his horse had already passed. Perhaps, he thought with growing concern, Mr. Varner had kept his threat and turned the young saddle horse out. Perhaps someone had seen Dusty and had stolen him!

Russ and his folks had been so confused and upset since Chuck's death that they had not concerned themselves with anything. If Dusty had been stolen the thieves could have hauled him a thousand miles away and sold him, and Russ would not even have known he was gone.

The lithe, muscular boy quickened his pace and was almost at the barn when Dianne came out on the kitchen porch and called to him. He turned hesitantly, keeping a wary eye for her father.

"I came to get Dusty and go see if I can find a place to keep him," he said lamely. "Is he all right?"

"He's fine." Her smile winked. "Daddy asked me to talk to you if he didn't get to see you."

"I haven't been able to look for a place to keep my horse," Russ continued, "but now that—" his voice choked— "now that things will be quieting down I—I'll find something right away."

"That's just it," she said, smiling. "Since Chuck's accident Dad has changed his mind."

Her words did not register with him immediately. He was not sure he fully understood what she meant.

She must have seen the questions in his eyes.

"You don't have to take your horse someplace else. After your brother got killed Dad got to thinking about what he had told you and decided that he was being unreasonable, so he asked me to tell you that you can still keep Dusty here, if you want to."

Russ Masters stared at her incredulously. It was still difficult to believe that a man like Mr. Varner would change his mind.

10

Russ went into the house with Dianne and talked to her and her mother briefly before excusing himself to go out to the barn and feed Dusty. He tried to thank them for allowing him to keep his horse at their place, but when he tried to speak about it he felt his throat choking and tears filling his eyes.

"You don't have to thank us," Dianne told him. "Having Dusty around is no bother at all. And I know Daddy appreciated your help."

"It was an answer to prayer," Mrs. Varner added, her eyes glistening. "Dianne's father is a good man—a wonderful man! But he's stubborn and not easily persuaded to do something he has set his mind against. God is the only one I know who could accomplish anything with him in that department."

"Mother!" Dianne protested, disapproval edging her voice. "You shouldn't say things like that about Daddy."

"Why not? It's true. If you ask your father he'll tell you, himself, that he's a stubborn man. He boasts that he has an opinion about everything and never changes his mind."

Russ was scarcely listening. The reason Mr. Varner changed his mind did not matter. All he cared about was getting to keep Dusty close by so he could feed and water him easily and get over to ride him whenever he wanted to.

Russ blurted another thank-you and fled the house, blinking back the tears. *Why had God softened Mr. Varner's heart?* he wondered. The boy knew that he did not have any right to ask *Him* for anything. He was not a Christian. He was a big phony, a faker who pretended to love Christ and trust Him for salvation so his folks and the preachers and Sunday school teachers would stay off his back.

Of course, Mrs. Varner was a believer now, he reasoned. God could have answered her prayers. She talked as though she had been praying that her husband would relent and allow Russ to keep Dusty at their farm.

Emotions churning, the Masters boy went over and patted Dusty on the nose, talking to him softly. Yet, he was not thinking about his quarter horse. His mind was back in the gym at school and the message Pastor Orman had brought.

He did not know why he had never heard a sermon like that before. He had certainly been in church often enough. But now that he thought about it, he did not think he had even heard the way of salvation explained. It was as though he had been wearing both blinders and ear plugs the other times Pastor Orman explained what a person had to do to be saved.

He knew his folks and the church did not believe that anyone could be good enough on his own and do enough good works to be worthy of going to heaven. He remembered hearing them quote Bible verses that said the only way to heaven was by trusting Jesus Christ for salvation. But he had closed his mind to that. He kept telling himself that he was good enough to make it on his own. He did not think he had anything to worry about. And, when he was a lot older and had lived a good share of his life, he would take a good look at the way things stacked up. If he saw, then, that he was not going to make it, after he had done all the things he wanted to do, he would become a Christian.

Until Saturday night's accident when Chuck had been killed, that had been his plan. Now he was not so sure things would work out that way. What if his older brother had not been a Christian at the time of the accident? His life would have been snuffed out, and he would not have had a chance to receive the Lord before he died. That was enough to make a guy think.

As Pastor Orman said at the funeral that afternoon, a guy ought to put his trust in Christ while he was young. Then he would be sure of going to heaven, regardless of when death came to him. And if he lived until he was old, he would have had an entire lifetime of service for God.

The truth of that thought was not new to Russ. He had heard his folks speak about it on numerous occasions when a young person received Christ as his Savior. And there were times when he had heard them lament the fact that someone else had waited until he was old to trust Christ for salvation, wasting most of the years God had given him in careless, selfish living. Thoughts of the opportunity to serve God and the uncertainty of life, which made the postponement of a decision to follow the Lord exceedingly dangerous, churned wildly through his heart.

More important, however, was the firm assurance that there was nothing he could do that would have pleased Chuck more than for him to give his heart and his life to Christ. He had seen the pain in his brother's handsome features when he refused to go to a youth retreat or evangelistic meetings at church. Chuck did not voice his

86

disappointment, and at the time it would not have made any difference if he had. But Russ *knew* how he felt. Now doing something that would have pleased his older brother was all-important.

Still, he knew that he could not receive Christ because it would have pleased Chuck, or his folks, or Pastor Orman, or anyone else. If he was going to become a Christian, it had to be on his own and because he wanted Christ for himself.

He pulled in a deep breath, looked about to be sure that he was alone, and dropped to his knees. He had prayed before when he wanted something he thought he might have trouble getting, like Dusty, or when he had a big test coming up and had not studied as hard as he should have. He had even prayed briefly the night the officer came to the house and told them about the car accident, asking God to keep the news about his brother from being true. But this was the first time he had ever opened his heart to God, asking Him to come into his life, cleansing him from sin and making him the sort of person he ought to be.

He asked God to forgive him for being so rebellious and headstrong and for all of his pretending to be a Christian when he knew it was not true. That afternoon he realized that he must have been just about the biggest hypocrite in the whole school—perhaps in the whole town.

He wondered if God would forgive him for having deceived his folks and the pastors and the people at church, making them think he walked with Christ when he knew he did not. Yet he knew what the Bible said about that. God had even saved Saul who had gone around Palestine killing Christians and made him into the apostle Paul. Russ knew that all he had to do was to mean business with God and He would forgive him.

When he finished praying Russ got to his feet self-consciously. His first thought was that he had sure made a fool of himself this time, but as it came to mind he knew it was not true. Satan had sent it to confuse and bewilder him. This was actually the first time he could hold his head up and speak the truth when he told anyone that he was a Christian. If anyone laughed at him for it, they would have to laugh.

He finished taking care of Dusty and was about to leave the barn by the door that opened toward the house when he checked himself and went out the back. He did not want Dianne to see him leave and come out to talk to him. He could not talk to her or anyone else right then.

One day he would tell her what he had done. For some reason he felt that she had to know, even though she was not a Christian and said that she did not want to be. But he did not think he could do it right then. He had to wait—to sort out his thoughts and let his heart stop pounding so hard.

Russ cut across the pasture. He was not sure, but he thought his folks might still be at the church. When he left they acted as though they were reluctant to go back to the house and be alone. In the church basement they had moved from one group of people to another, talking about trivialities, anything to keep their minds off the death of their son.

But when Russ got home from Varners' the family car was in the garage and his folks were alone. The last of their friends and relatives had left. Through the big window in the family room Russ saw his mother and dad sitting in front of the fireplace. A log was smoldering on the grate. His throat choked convulsively, and he felt the warmth of a tear on his cheek.

While he stood in the deepening shadows, he saw his mother get the big scrapbook in which she had recorded Chuck's athletic exploits. She sat down beside his dad and together they thumbed the pages slowly—lovingly.

As he had hurried across the dry grass of the pasture a few moments before, he had decided to go into the house and tell them that he was a Christian now, but as he saw them his resolve melted. How could he do that, he decided, when they already thought he was a believer? How could he speak of his faith in Christ when he did not know whether he could live up to what was expected of a Christian? He had been a hypocrite far too long. He was not going to be one again if he could help it.

"Come on in," his dad said with new tenderness. "We were just looking at Chuck's old scrapbook."

Russ sauntered in and slouched in a chair near the fire. He felt that he ought to say something, but he did not know what.

"I'm so glad Mom put this book together while things were happening for Chuck. I'd completely forgotten a lot of this stuff. We'd never have remembered it again if we didn't have these clippings to remind us." His smile was slow and trembling. "Y'know, Russ, Chuck was a great athlete. A really great athlete!"

The younger boy nodded. "He was a great brother, too."

"And a fine Christian son," Mrs. Masters added.

They continued to look at the thick book of clippings and pictures.

"Remember when this was taken?" she asked, pointing to a snapshot of Chuck in bed with the mumps.

"Do I?" Mr. Masters echoed. "It was only last year and seems as though it was last week. He took sick the night before the regional track meet, and we lost all three of his events. If he'd been out there, we'd have won the championship."

Russ recalled the incident, too. When the doctor told his older brother he could not compete, tears came to Chuck's eyes. It was the first time Russ had seen him cry since he was a kid and lost at checkers.

"I was just telling Mom that the next time she goes to town she could get a scrapbook just like this for you, Russ," his dad said, suddenly.

The boy's gaze widened. "What'd I ever do that would be good enough to get my picture in the paper?"

"Maybe you haven't yet," Mr. Masters said, confidently, "but you will. You're going to take Chuck's place. We've still got some empty spots in the record books and on Chuck's trophy shelf."

Russ glanced up, his gaze fixed uneasily on his dad. He was not sure he liked the trend the conversation was taking.

"I could *never* do the things Chuck's done," he muttered in protest.

"Don't say that," his father admonished. "You can do a lot more than you think. Just this afternoon at the church after the funeral Coach Anson told me that he's sure you're a second Chuck coming up. Russ, he's looking to you to be his starting quarterback."

Russ Masters should have been thrilled by the information about the coach's confidence in his ability. He knew his parents were and expected him to be. But he was not. Icy fear knotted his stomach and tightened bands of steel about his chest until his breath came in thin, shallow gasps.

"Anson thinks you ought to go to that sports camp Chuck went to the last couple of years. It'll help sharpen your ball

90

handling and teach you a few tricks the pros use. Sound OK?''

Russ winced, hesitating.

"OK?" his dad repeated.

"Oh, sure," he said, trying hard to sound more excited than he was. "It sounds great."

"Good. I told Anson to mail me the registration forms. We'll have to get you signed up right away or you might not get in. They've got a waiting list half a mile long."

"Maybe they're full already," Russ said, half hopefully.

"Anson said he'd guarantee you a place if we get your application in by the last of next week."

That night Russ tossed restlessly in bed. There was not any question about his going out for football the following August. There never had been. It was the least he could do for his brother and his folks. Even the people in town. It seemed to him that everyone expected him to be out for the team and be as good as Chuck. He knew they would expect it even more now that his brother had been killed. He swung his feet to the floor and sat up. Sweat moistened his forehead, and he wiped it away with a trembling hand. He was not Chuck, and he could never play football the way his older brother had. Not if he lived for a thousand years!

Still, he would *have* to try. He could not let his dad and mother down after they had gone through such agony.

He stood and moved to the window where he looked out over the yard toward the pasture where Dusty was kept. He would a lot rather be working with his horse than knocking himself out on the football field in an effort to be something he was not. But he did not have a choice.

Perhaps, with God's help and the athletic camp in Colorado that summer, he would learn that he had more ability at football than he thought he had. He hoped so, for the sake of his folks. For a long while he remained motionless at the window, praying.

11

It was different around the Masters house after Chuck's funeral service. From the time of his death until after his burial and the lunch at the church, people were coming and going constantly. Now all of that was over. People had gone back to their own affairs, pushing thoughts of Chuck and his family to the far reaches of their minds. Russ and his parents were left completely alone.

A shroud of melancholy and gloom settled over the house. Only a month earlier the family had been happy and carefree, inviting people in and being invited out whenever there was a free night. Now they did not go out at night, even if they were invited, and did not think of having anyone in. They did not feel like it. Mostly they were alone with their grief and their memories.

Russ did not want to be resentful of Chuck for his ability and the way people around town idolized him. That was especially true now that Chuck was dead. But the younger boy could not help the turmoil and occasional bitterness that swirled and eddied within his heart. Everywhere he turned someone was reminding him of Chuck's great natural talent and the difficulty Russ would have in measuring up to him.

It seemed to Russ that Chuck's ability and exploits grew every day in the telling and retelling. Fans talked now as

93

though the older Masters boy never called the wrong play or got sacked by the opposing line or was smeared behind the line of scrimmage. They were saying that he never lost his temper and never got frustrated or talked back to the referees. Those things had not happened very often with his older brother, he admitted, but they had happened. He had seen them, himself. He had even seen Chuck ejected from a game one time, but by now everyone had forgotten about that. In their eyes he was perfect. Russ not only had to compete against the real-life Chuck, who had set more athletic records than any other athlete in the history of the school. He now had to compete against a legend—the perfect student and athlete Chuck had never been.

He could not talk to his folks about it, he decided. They might think he had not cared about Chuck; that he did not want to go out for football or do any of the things his older brother excelled in. And he did. He did! It was just that he was already doomed to failure. He was not even half as good as Chuck was. He could hear the wagging tongues when he went out on the field with the varsity next fall and the fans got a good look at him and what he could do.

He knew what they would think and say. Russ Masters was 'dogging' it. He wasn't really trying to give his best— now, when Chuck was out there he didn't lie down and let the opposition walk over him. He gave his team everything he had, sparking them to play better than they ever would without him!

Because Russ's name was Masters, no one in town would admit that he did not have all the natural talent of his older brother. Any shortcomings in the way he produced would be because he did not try hard enough—because he did not care!

He clenched his fists and paced back and forth across his room, quietly, for his dad was watching the news on TV a short distance away. Russ did not want to have to answer a lot of questions about what he was doing and why. He did not want to be told that Chuck had never done anything so foolish.

He had already made his decision, and he would go through with it the best he knew how. He was out for track because his dad insisted on it, and he would go to the athletic camp in July. He would work as hard as he could at being everything he was expected to be, but even as he made those promises to himself, he knew that they would not be enough. No matter how hard he tried, he could never master the game well enough to make his dad proud of him.

Suddenly his anger flared. Now his folks had that stupid scrapbook they were waiting for him to fill with his football and basketball exploits. *I could have told them it's a waste of money,* he thought, bitterly. That was one scrapbook that was sure not to get used!

The stable his dad was having built for Dusty should have been finished in a couple of weeks, but the carpenter took a spill on his motorcycle and was in the hospital for a time. When he was finally released, it was with the stern admonition not to go to work again until the doctor decided he was able. Not that it mattered. Mr. Varner did not say anything more to Russ about moving his horse. In fact, save for the hard glint of steel in his eyes when his wife mentioned studying the Bible or being friends with Russ's mother, it would have seemed that nothing had changed. He still joked with Russ when he saw him and let him know that he was expecting him to come back to work when school was out.

It would have suited Russ to have started working on the farm any time, only there were not enough extra hours in the day to add working to his busy schedule. With track and his studies and other activities to keep up he did not have the time he wanted to spend with Dusty. He got over to take care of his young gelding every night and occasionally was able to squeeze in a couple of hours of riding, either alone or with Dianne, but that was all. She teased him about having been out of the saddle so long he would have to learn to ride all over again, or he might have to break Dusty a second time.

"It'll be better after school's out," he said lamely. "I'll have more time to ride then."

"I thought you were supposed to have time this spring as soon as it got warm," she chided. "We were going to start roping again, remember?"

The muscles in his jaw tightened, and he looked beyond her at the hills on the far horizon.

"It's that stupid track," he muttered, more to himself than to Dianne. "It'll be over in another month. Then I'll have time to do a lot of things."

She glanced his direction, her eyes narrowing. "Don't you *like* being out for track?"

He paused uneasily. At least once before he had mentioned to her his feelings about track and got a violent reaction. He wished he had not said anything this time. She would not goad him about it again.

"Don't you like being out for track?" she repeated.

"I've done things I've liked a lot more," he admitted.

She shook her head incredulously and, gathering up her mount's reins, turned him so she could face her companion. "If you don't *like* being out for track," she retorted, "why

96

do you do it? That's what I can't figure out.''

He did not answer her immediately, and she repeated the question.

"You know the answer to that,'' he retorted petulantly. "You don't have to ask.''

"Maybe I do,'' she told him. "But you wouldn't catch me doing something if I didn't want to.'' She shook her head. "I don't understand you.''

"You don't have to understand!'' he said, bluntly, riding away. Right then he would not have cared if Dianne had turned and galloped her horse over the greening pasture to the barn. She had no reason to tell him what he ought to do. She did not know anything about the pressure he faced.

She seemed to sense that she had gone as far as she dared. "Come on!'' she cried, changing the subject quickly. "I'll race you to the lane!''

Russ whirled Dusty and drove his heels into the lean young gelding's flanks. "You're on!'' And they went pounding over ground not yet softened by spring rains. They galloped into the lane at a dead heat, laughing happily. They stopped at the house for some hot chocolate and cookies with Mrs. Varner before continuing their ride.

Russ wanted to cross the pasture and take a look at the new young stock Mr. Varner had brought home from the last quarter horse sale in Denver, but Dianne had other ideas. She insisted that they go to the fairgrounds. She insisted so strongly that he gave in and together they rode in the ditch along the graveled road to the fairgrounds where the saddle club had their chutes and holding pens and kept their rodeo rough stock.

"We're going to start working out in a couple of weeks,'' Dianne said, glancing obliquely in his direction.

He studied the calves wistfully.

"How about joining us?"

"That would be great!"

"Then, you will?" she asked, eagerly.

Clouds crossed his young face, and his lower lip trembled slightly. "I'd like to," he told her, "but I don't think I can work it out."

Her gaze pierced his. "You can't work it out," she snapped, "or your folks won't let you work it out?"

"They don't have a thing to do with it!" he exploded. "I do as I please!"

That was not true, of course. He had lied to Dianne. The instant the words left his lips he was ashamed of what he had said. But he could not help it. He could not have a *girl* making fun of him. Even one like Dianne.

"If you can do as you please," she persisted, "and you *really* want to join the saddle club so you can work out with us and enter some of the rodeos, why don't you?"

He hesitated. "I—I'll think about it."

She laid a hand on his arm, impulsively. "We need you, Russ," she told him. "And I *know* it's what you want to do."

The day of Chuck's funeral, when Russ had become a Christian, he vowed that he would tell Dianne what he had done. On two or three occasions he tried, but didn't succeed very well. She did not understand much of what he was trying to say, for one thing. For another, she didn't want to.

"Now you're beginning to sound like my mom!" she said curtly. "If Dad finds out that you're preaching to me, too, he'll make you move Dusty."

98

"I'm going to move him anyway," he said, "next week."

Hurt flecked her eyes, and her fingers loosed momentarily on the reins. "You don't have to, you know," she said, quietly.

"The stable's about finished, and I think it would be better to have him over home where I can take care of him easier."

She pulled in a deep breath. "I suppose you're right," she agreed, but the tone of her voice said that she really did not want him to take Dusty away from their place.

"But I'll still come over and help you work on your barrel racing and goat tying," he said, "that is, if you want me to."

She nodded, smiling.

For an instant he thought he saw tears in her eyes, and he flushed uncomfortably. He did not know what was the matter with her. One minute she was taunting him as though she wished she would never see him again. Now this. He sure could not figure out girls! Nothing they said or did seemed to make sense.

Then, quite unexpectedly, she slapped her horse across the back with her hand and raced off, shouting challenges to Russ. He followed, crouching low on Dusty's back and urging him faster and faster. But it was no use. Dianne's lead was too long, and she beat him handily. And when the race was over, she was her own happy self again.

Russ took Dusty home to the new stable the following weekend, thinking that he would get more time to ride, having his horse at home. But it did not work out that way.

Every time he planned to go for a ride something came up to keep him from it.

Things were a little better after school was out and he started helping Mr. Varner again. He worked with Dianne on her goat tying and barrel racing and threw a few loops, himself, at Varner's calves. He did not dare do too much of it, or he would risk upsetting Dianne's dad.

"You ought to join the saddle club," she told him. "Then you could rope their stock all you want to."

He grinned at her. "I've been thinking on it."

"I've got an application any time you decide you want to fill it out."

"I'll remember that."

Russ went to the athletic camp in Colorado that summer and was out for football at Platte Valley High the week before school started. Coach Anson treated him the way he did the rest of the guys, but the local sportswriter did a piece on him. NEW STAR AT P.V. HIGH? the headline asked.

The story was fair enough, he supposed. The reporter had recounted Chuck's successes and his tragic death. Then he wrote of Russ, who was expected to fill his brother's position and carry on in what had become the great Masters tradition. Yet, it irritated him. Why couldn't they let him alone? Why did they have to keep badgering him about all the things Chuck had done? Did they not realize that he was not Chuck and could never be like him? When he read a piece like that he wanted to find a hole and crawl into it.

Russ did not get to start the first two games, and he knew that disappointed his parents terribly. But there was nothing he could do about it. He had given the position everything he had, and it still was not good enough. Chuck's backup, Jerry Knoedler, had too much experience for him. Russ had

100

played most of the second quarter and part of the third, but at that point it should have been obvious to everyone, he reasoned, that Jerry was going to lead the team.

He was surprised to learn how kind the fans and the local paper were to him. People stopped him on the street and told him how glad they were that he was out for football. They gave excuses for him now, saying he was young and inexperienced.

"Wait and see," they told him, "you'll be as good as Chuck was before the year's over."

He was glad for their confidence in his ability, but he also found it disturbing. What would they think and say when they learned the truth about how poorly he played?

No one knew that Jerry had hurt his knee in the second game until the final gun sounded and they were on their way to the locker room. Coach Anson saw that Jerry was limping and insisted on calling in a doctor to examine him. The report was just as the coach expected. The starting quarterback would be out of the next two games at least, and perhaps for the rest of the season.

"Well, Russ," the coach said, turning toward the young substitute, "it looks as though it's going to be up to you."

The boy stared at him numbly, not knowing what the coach meant.

"You'll be running the team next Friday night!" the coach continued, patting him reassuringly on the shoulder.

Both elated and frightened, Russ went out to the car where his parents were waiting for him. He was happy for the chance to start because it would please the folks, but he was afraid, too. In the first two games he had had Jerry to fall back on. That had made a big difference in his confidence. Now all he had to take over if he got into trouble was a quarterback with even less experience than he had.

On the way home, after his dad had gone over his time in the game, play by play, he told them that he would be starting the game the following Friday.

"That's great!" his dad said.

"It certainly is," Mrs. Masters added. "I was just sitting here thinking about Chuck. He started every football game he ever played in and was All State his first year."

Russ winced and turned away. The joy was gone.

12

Russ's spirits were leaden as he worked out with the team the following week. The first two sessions everything seemed to go wrong. Linemen missed their assignments and backs stumbled over each other as they attempted to run the simplest of plays. The second string defense forced them to punt three times in a row and on the last almost blocked the kick.

Coach Anson was pacing back and forth along the sidelines, more nervous and concerned than Russ had seen him all year. Nobody said anything, but the Masters boy knew the source of most of the bewilderment and confusion. It was he. He was as taut as a guitar string and as clumsy as a newborn calf. When the Tuesday afternoon practice was over the coach called him aside.

"What's the problem?" he asked, keeping his voice down.

"Problem?" He tried to pretend that he did not understand. "What do you mean?"

"You're not playing the way you did Friday night.

"I—I thought I was doing OK," Russ lied.

"Well, you weren't. If you play this Friday the way you have yesterday and today, we're beaten before we start."

Russ moistened his lips with the tip of his tongue. "I—I—"

"You've got to relax, Russ," he went on. "When you choke up that way you can't execute plays properly and you can't pass."

He nodded. "I guess I have been uptight."

"You can say that again." There was a brief pause. "Now, this is what I want you to do. Go home tonight and forget all about football. Forget about our practice this afternoon and the practice tomorrow. If you can, make yourself think that you won't be playing again for six months."

Russ did not see what good that would do, but he was willing to try.

"After school, when you come out for practice I don't want you to think about the fact that you're starting Friday night. Forget about the consequences of making a mistake during the game. Come out on the field as loose and carefree as you would if you and some of the guys were in a game of softball in the pasture behind your folks' house. OK?"

"OK."

The following afternoon football practice went much better. Russ was not completely relaxed and during the course of the scrimmage made two or three bobbles that would have cost them good yardage in the course of a regular game. In spite of that, however, the offensive team began to fuse together, and, equally important, the rest of the players began to recognize Russ's position of leadership. The practice went well, and Coach Anson was greatly encouraged.

On Friday night Russ took charge of the Platte Valley offensive unit, sparking them to a 14-7 lead in the first half and a 31-19 victory. There had been one series of downs midway in the second quarter when Russ seemed to lose control, and two illegal procedure penalties back-to-back made it necessary for him to punt. Other than that he was the master of the situation, running the team with assurance and ease.

A warm glow enveloped him as he left the field with his teammates when the game was over. Chuck would have done a smoother job, there was no doubt of that. Mr. Masters always said that Chuck had executed his plays with confidence seldom seen at the high school level. Yet the younger Masters boy had nothing to be ashamed of. He knew he had done a good job. He wished Chuck could have been there to have seen it.

At home later in the evening his dad questioned him the way he used to question Chuck following a game. He wanted to know why certain plays had been called in a given situation and what Coach Anson thought of PV's chances of winning the next two games.

". . . they're both going to be tough," he concluded. "A lot tougher than Pine Bluffs was tonight."

"That's what the coach told us."

"You'll have to give it everything you've got, if you're going to be able to take your brother's place." Russ clamped his lips tightly together and said nothing, but his cheeks flushed and resentment bristled within. It seemed to him that his dad was trying to say that he did not think he had quite enough ability to handle the rest of the schedule.

"I was proud of what you did tonight, Russ," Mr. Masters said at last. "You're going to have to play a lot better next week than you did tonight to pull out another victory, but I think you can do it. Chuck used to say, 'We only play one game at a time.' And that's the way it is now. One game at a time. Tonight it was Pine Bluffs. Next week it's Baker.''

Russ did not remember what he had said to his dad after that. All he knew was that the ache in his stomach grew. Winning that night had not been enough to prove himself. He had another game to play, and another, and another.

The following morning Russ rode Dusty over to the Varner place to help Dianne's dad. He did not know the outcome of the game the night before and did not care. And that was fine with Russ. He would just as soon forget about football, at least for a while.

An hour or so later Mr. Varner got in his pickup and went to town for a load of oats and the next week's supply of groceries. Dianne came out as soon as he left the yard and asked Russ to help her with her barrel racing.

"Sure thing," he said, indifferently. He was still thinking about the things his dad had said after the football game.

"I've been practicing at the fairgrounds with the saddle club," she said, "and my time's improving a lot."

"We'll see just how well you're doing," he told her.

"If you don't believe me, just watch!" She mounted her horse and guided him back to the starting line.

"When you're ready say the word, and I'll give you the sign to start."

Shadow fiddlefooted nervously. As Russ's hand came down, the powerful horse leaped forward into a dead run. He stretched out across the hard ground, pounding toward the first barrel. Dianne leaned expertly into the turn, guiding her mount with her knees and a slight pressure on the reins.

He came out of the turn and sped for the second barrel faster than Russ had ever seen him move in that particular race before. When Dianne crossed the finish line after circling the third barrel the Masters boy whistled his amazement.

"What was the time?" she asked, riding back to where he was standing.

"Nineteen and two fifths seconds," he exclaimed.

"I told you I was getting better."

"I didn't think you were that much better."

She swung off her mount and stood beside him. "You could do the same, Russ," she said, "if you would only join the saddle club so you could work out every week."

"I'll think about it," he said without enthusiasm. Even as he spoke he knew that would not do any good. He would never be able to do it.

The first half of the game with Baker was disastrous for both Russ and Platte Valley. In the opening minutes of the game the young quarterback had two passes intercepted that resulted in a touchdown and a field goal. And in the second half he gave a hand-off to the wrong man and lost fifteen yards that effectively stopped a drive that began on their own 18-yard line and ended with a missed field goal on the Baker 22.

In the rest of the third quarter things went a little better for the home team, and they put 7 points on the board. But that was not enough. They lost 10 to 7.

Russ was disconsolate as he rode home with his folks that night. His dad tried to ease his hurt, but his own disappointment showed through so keenly anything he said only made his son feel worse than he did already.

When they reached the house Russ went directly to his room and closed the door. His dad's words were ringing in his ears. No matter how hard he tried, he could not do it. He had failed his folks, miserably. He knelt beside his bed and asked forgiveness for making such a mess of things. Then he asked God to help him to be good enough so his parents and the kids at school would not be ashamed of him. Yet, when he finished, the same gnawing ache filled his very being.

The next morning he got up at the usual time, but stayed in his bedroom until he was sure his mother and dad would have finished breakfast. When he came out he was surprised to see them still at the table with Pastor Orman in the chair where Chuck used to sit. Both the minister and Mr. Masters were wearing flannel shirts and jeans tucked into the tops of their low-cut boots. Their hunting coats were thrown over the back of a straight-backed chair in the corner, and their shotguns stood nearby.

"Hi," Russ said with an enthusiasm he did not feel. "Looks like you guys are going hunting."

"We're not getting around very fast today," his dad replied. "We should have been out of here two hours ago. I guess last night's game was too much for us."

The boy turned away, quickly.

"We were just talking about you, Russ," the pastor said, his smile warm and inviting. "How'd you like to go with us?"

He hesitated, looking from one to the other. They used to take Chuck hunting with them every pheasant season, but this was the first time they had ever asked him. He had planned on going over to Varners' to go riding with Dianne, but this was great. After breakfast he phoned and told her that he would not be there until the middle of the afternoon.

The trio went north of town several miles to some cornfields that belonged to a member of the church and

108

started to walk the long rows, their guns cradled in their arms. Mr. Masters took the far position, placing Pastor Orman between himself and Russ. Not until later did the significance of that arrangement become apparent to the boy. He had seen it as a coincidence—as one of those things that just happens—until Pastor Orman worked his way over to him and suggested that they stop to rest.

"Sure," Russ said, quickly. "I'll call Dad."

"Oh, don't do that. I—as a matter of fact, I'd like to talk to you alone."

Then Russ saw it all, or thought he did. The decision of his dad and Pastor Orman to go hunting on Saturday, their sitting around the table until he got up, and the invitation to him to go along. They had not wanted him with them because they enjoyed his company, he told himself. He was sure they asked him to join them so the pastor could have a chance to talk to him. He felt his cheeks grow hot, and he wanted to throw down the shotgun and storm back to town on foot. Why would his dad ask the minister to talk to him? Did he think he had thrown the Baker game on purpose? In calmer moments he would have known that was not the reason, if his dad had planned it, but he was so confused and bewildered that morning he had to have something to blame his problems on.

"I'm glad you came along," the minister began. "We used to have some good hunting trips with Chuck."

"I know," he retorted cryptically.

"You remember I talked with you about the example he had left for you to follow?"

Russ murmured his assent. It did not sound as though the minister was even going to mention the football game, and that both surprised and reassured him. He remembered the conversation Pastor Orman was talking about. He had stopped in to the pastor's study a couple of weeks after the funeral to tell the minister about his own decision to let Christ rule his life, but the minister had voiced such assurance that he was a Christian, he had not dared.

"We talked about Chuck's testimony for Christ and the way he led the other kids."

"I know."

"I told you then that you would be able to have the same influence as your brother on the kids at school. Now that you're the starting quarterback, you're in the same position Chuck was."

"After last night?" Russ demanded bitterly.

"After last night. Everybody has problems like that."

"Chuck didn't."

"I'm sure Chuck had times when he felt as though he was a terrible failure. In fact I've talked with him when he was that way, after a game he thought didn't go as well as it should, or if something went wrong in the youth group at church. The thing I want to stress is this. The kids at school will listen to you the same way they listened to your brother. You'll be able to lead them—to influence them to make a decision for Jesus Christ."

The muscles in his throat constricted, and he felt the sweat grow cold on his forehead. He had not expected the minister to admit that Chuck had problems at times, and he sure had not thought he would say that Russ could have an influence on the other kids at school. He sounded almost like Mr. Masters, except that his dad would never admit that Chuck had ever stubbed his toe at anything.

"I—I don't know about that," he said, uncertainly.

"You're too modest, Russ. The kids will follow you the

110

way they did Chuck. I just wanted to tell you I still believe that, in spite of the game last night, and I'm praying that God will help you to take over where Chuck left off.''

The Masters boy kicked a clod with his foot. He wanted to talk to Pastor Orman about the whole situation, to tell him how helpless he felt when he even thought about filling his brother's shoes. There was no way he could be what Chuck had been on the football field or off. He was not made like his brother. He could not do things the way Chuck did. Couldn't they see that?

His heart cried out for help, but there was no one who would listen. And there was no way that he could measure up to the standards they tried to make him accept. The hurt deepened as he listened to the kindly voice of the minister.

The three of them spent the entire morning hunting and got four birds, but for Russ the rest of the trip was torturous. Even his dad and Pastor Orman saw how quiet he was and asked the reason for it. But, of course, he could not tell them. How could he, when he knew they would not understand?

Toward mid-afternoon he went over to Varners' on Dusty. Dianne was in the barn when he got there, currying her quarter horse. She, too, had something she wanted to talk with him about. She had mentioned his joining the saddle club several times before, so he could get the experience he needed to make the high school rodeo team. Now she insisted on it.

''You could work out with us this fall and be ready to try out in the spring,'' she said. ''And you'd make it. That I'd guarantee.''

He hesitated, studying her attractive young features

111

thoughtfully. Joining the saddle club and roping their calves sounded great to him, but he did not think it was possible. "I'm already out for football," he told her. "When would I have time to practice roping?"

"Saturdays," she answered quickly. "The games are on Friday night, and the football squad *never* practices on the day after a game."

He wanted to. How he wanted to. But there was no way he could do it. He knew what his dad would say if he asked him.

"You can't handle them at the same time, Russ," he would explain impatiently. "And if you try, you'll wind up neglecting one or the other, or being lousy in both. You never saw Chuck take on any other athletic project during the football season, did you? That was because he had his priorities straightened out. He kept his eye on the ball."

Russ directed his attention back to Dianne. "I don't think I can," he told her, lamely.

Her eyes flashed, and her voice was harsh with scorn. "What's the matter? Won't your dad let you?"

He squirmed uneasily. "That's not it," he blurted.

She refused to accept his denial. "You want to join the saddle club, don't you?" she persisted.

He had to admit that he did.

"Then the only reason you don't is because of your dad," she continued, triumphantly. "He won't let you!"

"He doesn't have anything to do with it!" Russ exploded. "I do as I please!"

"Then prove it!"

He hadn't figured on the situation taking a turn like that. "I've got to be going."

"It'll only take ten minutes to fill out the form. You're not in *that* big a hurry, are you?"

"I guess not."

"Then come on in the kitchen, and we'll get it taken care of. I've got the application blanks in my room."

He tied Dusty to a rail near the water tank and reluctantly followed Dianne into the house. He hoped that Mrs. Varner was there to stop what was happening, but she was lying down, so there was nothing he could do except to go through with it. At least, that was the way it seemed to him.

Once they started on the form he was excited about the prospects of being a member of the saddle club. He knew what his dad would say if he found out, but he did not figure on letting him know. And besides, he could not have Dianne thinking he was not able to make his own decisions.

Filling out the form was only a matter of a few minutes. He told Dianne what to write in reply to the questions, and she set the answers to the paper. They were almost finished when she stopped suddenly and exclaimed aloud.

"What's the matter?" he demanded.

"Your folks are supposed to sign this. I'd forgotten all about that." She looked down at the application once more. "Now I remember asking Dad about it when I joined," she continued. "He said the parents of all minors have to sign that if their son or daughter gets hurt using the rough stock that belongs to the saddle club, or if they would happen to get hurt on a sponsored trail ride, they wouldn't sue the club."

Russ tried to mask his relief. He actually had wanted to join the saddle club, but he had not wanted to go against the wishes of his parents. Now he would not have to, and he would not have Dianne uptight with him about it.

"I guess that takes care of that." He pushed himself away from the table.

113

"You don't think your folks would sign for you?" she asked, disappointed, as disappointed as Russ was relieved.

He shook his head. "No way. Chuck didn't belong to the saddle club," he added bitterly, "so I'm not supposed to, either."

Dianne frowned and muttered under her breath. Then her eyes brightened, and she got quickly to her feet.

"You wait here!" she exclaimed. "I'll take care of everything."

A few moments later she was back, waving the application like a banner of victory. "Well, I've got it!" she exclaimed. "All signed and everything."

Russ Masters' eyes widened. "How can you say that?" he demanded, skeptically.

"Because I got it signed, that's why."

He still could not believe her. "You'd have had to work a miracle to get my dad to sign a paper like that. I mean it! He's death on anything that interferes with football."

"Maybe so," she told him, "but I got this paper signed. If you don't believe me, just take a look." She waved the paper under his nose.

He stared at her and then at the paper she held. "You sure rushed getting over to my place and back." Then a smile spread across his lean features. "You've got to be kidding, Dianne. You haven't had time to go to our house, let alone talk Dad into signing this application and getting back here."

"Who said anything about going to your place?" she asked. "I talked our new hired hand into signing it."

Russ stared at her. "You what?"

"It's just a formality," she continued. "And no one will ever know about it! Nobody's *ever* been hurt in all the years

114

of the saddle club!'' She folded the application and inserted it in an envelope. ''I'll have Dad give me five dollars out of your next wages, and we'll be all set! You're going to say that this is the best thing you've ever done after you've been in the club for a while!''

13

Monday afternoon Jerry Knoedler was out for practice the first time since his injury, and Coach Anson put him in as quarterback on the starting eleven. Russ could not blame him for that after the way he had loused things up in the Baker game. Still, the emptiness he felt trotting off the field Friday night seized him again.

He could not quite understand himself. He resented being pushed into Chuck's mold and tried to say that he did not particularly like football, but it hurt to blow a game the way he had the Baker contest.

With a certain jealousy he watched Knoedler handle the team. It hurt to see the guys functioning as smoothly as a well-oiled machine. They were not playing against an outfit like Baker, he assured himself. They were playing the reserves. That made it easier for them to look sharp. Still, that did not eliminate his own dissatisfaction with the way he had played.

Jerry went down after the first series of plays and had to be helped off the field. Everyone crowded around him, concern stamped on their youthful faces. They did not want to see Jerry hurt, but Russ knew they were also thinking about something else. Like how poorly he had run the team their last time out and how badly they needed Knoedler.

The coach sent Russ in to take Jerry's place and called an assistant over. Moments later he saw the assistant coach call two guys out of the reserve backfield and talk with them. Russ recognized them at once. They were the guys who had tried out for the position the first of the season and had been beaten out. Now it looked as though they were going to get another opportunity.

He felt his lean torso tense. He'd show them, he promised himself darkly. He'd beaten them out once, and he'd do it again!

There was good news about Jerry when Russ got back to school the next morning. The other quarterback had strained an ankle instead of reinjuring his knee. He might be able to see limited duty in the Oak Ridge game, but he should be ready for the biggest contest of the year—the one with Granby, at Granby the following week.

"At full speed," was the way Coach Anson had described Jerry's expected condition for the Conference Championship game.

Russ bore down harder than he ever had in practice, and his concentration showed up in the way he executed the plays. There was no question in the minds of anyone who saw the squad scrimmaging that he would be starting on Friday night. One of the new quarterbacks was taken to Oak Ridge with the team, but even he was aware that, barring injuries, his chance of getting in was not good.

As far as Russ was concerned it was going to be a replica of the Baker game. He got into trouble at the start and was so shaky and uncertain Coach Anson had the new substitute warming up. Russ saw what was happening and got a grip on himself, completing two passes in a row and calling for an unexpected running play at third and nine that caught the

117

opposition flat-footed. Two well-placed blocks sprung the fullback for thirty-seven yards, and Platte Valley was knocking at Oak Ridge's front door. The drive continued until the ball was on the 6 yard line, and two more downs punched it across for the first TD of the night.

After that, Russ's play was somewhat erratic. For a while he operated smoothly with sharply executed moves, and they rolled up good yardage. About the time it looked as though they were going to score, he would bungle a play for no gain or a loss and the offense would begin to sputter. Platte Valley had three turnovers in the game, and Russ was directly responsible for two of them. On one occasion he fumbled, giving Oak Ridge the ball on the 8-yard line. Only an heroic stand by the defense held them to a field goal attempt that was promptly blocked to end the threat.

That seemed to take the life out of the opposing team. Where they were sharp and alert, they suddenly became dull and uncertain. Plays were broken without the help of Platte Valley, the center became inept in snapping the ball, and the punter kicked off the side of his foot on two occasions, sending the ball out of bounds before it had traveled twenty yards. It was one of those nights for Oak Ridge—a night both the fans and the team would have as soon forgotten.

Coach Anson sent Jerry Knoedler in briefly at the start of the third quarter, but he was limping after the first play, so he was jerked in favor of Russ. The Masters boy moved the ball downfield against a tired Oak Ridge eleven, scoring a second touchdown after a long series of plays that ground out yardage to eat up the clock. Such a precaution would not have been necessary. Their opponents were worn to the point where they had little fight left in them. Once or twice Oak Ridge mounted a feeble offense that showed a measure of promise, but the drive was finished after three or four plays. Backs fumbled the ball or ran into each other, linemen missed assignments, leaking tacklers that held them to six first downs in the entire game, and the quarterback threw desperately wild passes that were uncatchable.

When the game was over Russ was glad that he had been able to hold things together, but in his heart he knew that he had not played well enough to have been responsible for the victory, the way Chuck would have been. Even the substitute quarterback, who had not played a minute at that position in a regular game, could probably have defeated Oak Ridge the way they played that night.

Mr. and Mrs. Masters had reached home some time earlier, but were still up when the team returned from the neighboring town. They talked for a few minutes about the victory, but Russ knew that they were as aware as he was of his own uncertain, fumbling game. In all the time Chuck played he had never turned in a performance like that. Mr. Masters said little about the way his son had played, but saved most of his congratulations for the defensive unit.

That night in his room, getting ready for bed, Russ wondered how well he would be able to do when they met another tough team—like Granby—an outfit that would not let him make mistakes and get away with it.

Early Saturday morning Russ saddled Dusty and rode over to the Varner place. Dianne had stopped him in the hall at school the day before and told him that he was now a member of the local saddle club.

"They were going to send a notice in the mail, she said, giggling. "But I told them I'd see that you got it. We

119

wouldn't want your dad finding out so soon, would we?''

Russ flinched and directed his attention to his horse, quickly. He was certain that Dianne was going to keep on needling him, but she did not. She was much too excited about getting over to the fairgrounds to start working out.

''I've already told them you'd be there, roping,'' she said. ''Somebody'll help us get the calves in the chute if they're not already.''

''What I need,'' he told her, uneasily, ''is someone who can show me how to rope.''

''That can be arranged, too.''

When they reached the fairgrounds there were two other fellows about Russ's age or a bit younger practicing for the breakaway calf roping event. The calves were worked into place in the chute, and at a signal from the roper the gate was swung open. The calf raced out, the barrier went down, and the horse and rider exploded across the line in pursuit. Once within range, the whirling loop snaked out toward the hard-running animal. If the roper was lucky and the noose fell over the calf's bobbing head, he let it tighten slightly before dropping the free end of the lariat. A rider in the arena clocked his time with a stop watch.

On Russ's first try he missed the calf with both loops. The wiry little animal ran another twenty yards or so and slowed to a walk. He looked back disdainfully, as though to see what kind of roper had missed so far.

''Oh, man!'' Russ exclaimed, gathering in the second rope and dismounting to retrieve the first. ''There's no use in trying any more. I'll *never* be able to do it.''

''Don't feel that way,'' Dianne encouraged. ''You've got to remember it's been a long, long time since you've used a rope. It's only natural that you'd be rusty.''

"Rusty?" he echoed. "It looks like I've never had a lariat in my hands before today."

"Oh, it isn't as bad as all that. There was a time or two when you'd have roped him easily if the calf had only been cooperative."

"It's bad enough," he grumbled, shaking out another loop and twirling it absentmindedly while waiting for his turn. As the day wore on he began to show a certain proficiency not evident earlier. Most of his throws fell wide of their mark, but he did manage to get one on a calf's back, several inches behind the ears, and another fell across the running animal's nose. The calf shook it off without breaking stride. Russ counted them as 'near misses' and took credit for getting better. In an actual rodeo he knew that 'near misses' did not count, but that day he needed all the encouragement he could get.

At noon Russ and Dianne found a place in the warmth of the bright October sun where they could sit with several others and have lunch. They talked as they ate and afterward went back to working out.

Dianne was striving to sharpen her turns for barrel racing, and Russ was trying to learn to make a rope go where he wanted it to.

The afternoon was almost over when it happened. The sun had moved steadily downward toward the western horizon, and the wind gusted sharply across the arena, kicking up little puffs of dust. Russ noted the time and rode over to where Dianne was getting ready for another run, circling the barrels. They had been away all day. Although his folks knew he would be gone all morning and part of the afternoon, it was only normal that they would be curious about what he had been doing. The longer he stayed the more questions he was likely to face.

"About time to go home, Dianne?" he asked her.

"One more trial," she said, gathering the reins and swinging up into the saddle. "Things are going so well today I don't want to leave."

"If I have to stay here until things start going well for me I'll be around for a year."

She laughed at him and turned her mount back toward the starting line. There was nothing Russ could do except to wait. Even then, he planned to quit for the day, but there was one more calf in the chute, and he was the only breakaway roper still at the fairgrounds.

"Want him, Masters?" the man at the chute called, "or should I let him go?"

"I'll take him," he said, suddenly making up his mind.

The calf scooted out of the chute as the gate swung open, and Russ kicked Dusty in the flanks. The horse leaped to a dead run. By this time he sensed what he was to do and followed the calf. The wiry little creature veered sharply to the left and the quarter horse did the same. His left front hoof caught in a small hole, and he pitched forward, throwing Russ headlong to the ground.

Dusty staggered forward in a desperate effort to stay on his feet, but that was impossible. He stumbled again, as though the pain when he put his left hoof to the ground was unbearable. He crumpled, helplessly. For a moment or two after the fall Russ was motionlesss. Then he stirred, blinking his eyes. Riders crowded about him excitedly, demanding to know if he had been hurt.

"No," he murmered uncertainly. "I haven't been hurt. At least I don't think so."

He still lay there, shaking his head and trying to decide if there were any aches and pains that he was ignoring. His

122

shoulder throbbed, and his hip ached at the spot that first touched the ground. Gingerly he reached back and rubbed it.

Then he remembered his horse.

"What about Dusty?" he cried.

Raising himself on one arm he turned to stare at the injured animal.

"Dusty!" he cried, scrambling to his feet and staggering toward him. "Is he all right?"

"Take it easy," one of the men ordered, putting out an arm to restrain him.

Magnuson, one of the men who seemed to know more about horses than the rest, was on his knees beside the quivering animal, examining his leg, carefully. Russ crowded as close as he could and watched in silence.

"Think it's broken?" he asked at last, as though he was not sure he had the strength to accept the answer.

"I don't think so," Magnuson replied without looking up. "His leg is swollen, but not enough to indicate that it's broken. I'm sure he has a bowed tendon."

"H-how serious is that?" Russ asked.

"The chances are that putting him in the barn or in a pasture where there aren't any other horses to get him to running, would be enough to make him as good as new. It'll take some time to heal, if that's what it is, but it's not too serious."

"Maybe you ought to get the vet for him," Dianne suggested. "Just to be sure he doesn't have a broken bone or something like that."

The boy jerked erect. Doc Bell was a member of their church and a good friend of his dad's. If he was called, Russ was sure his folks would find out about Dusty getting hurt.

And when that happened he would be in real trouble. They wouldn't rest until they had learned the whole story about his joining the saddle club without permission or their signature and everything.

"What's the matter?" Dianne asked, curiously. "Don't you *want* Dr. Bell to examine Dusty?"

"I—I—" He moistened his lips with the tip of his tongue and tried to think of something to tell her without blurting the truth in front of everyone.

"I really don't know that it's necessary to have Bell look at him right now," Magnuson broke in, rescuing Russ. "At least I don't think it's necessary unless his leg gets worse. If it were my horse I'd take him home and watch him closely. I'd give him some exercise by walking him and see how he is in a day or two. If he doesn't get better soon I'd have the vet out."

The others were nodding confidently as Magnuson gave his opinion. The rest of the saddle club trusted the judgement of the wiry, bearded horseman, and that was enough for Russ. They all knew more about horses and taking care of them than he did, so he weighed what they said, carefully. Besides, following Magnuson's advice was better than taking his injured gelding to the vet until it was absolutely necessary.

"Want to use my horse trailer to haul him home?" Magnuson asked. Russ stared numbly at him. Home! That was right! He'd have to take the injured Dusty home! That meant his folks would still find out that the young gelding had been hurt and would have to know how and where it happened! *He was still in big trouble!*

14

Russ turned to Dianne in desperation. "Do—do you think we could keep Dusty over at your place for a while?" he blurted.

Her forehead crinkled quizzically. "Why?" she asked, curiously. "Any special reason?"

He swallowed hard. By this time he knew that his cheeks were scarlet. He was sure that everyone in the group was aware of his real reason for not wanting to take Dusty home. They *knew*, and the story would be all over town by Monday morning. Angrily he told himself that he was being foolish. Even Dianne would not know for sure.

She questioned him again about his reason for wanting to take his horse to their farm.

"B-because my dad—I mean your dad knows horses so well and everything. I—" The words choked off in an embarrassed silence. Now he had been so stupid they would know. He had practically told them.

But Magnuson—good old Magnuson—broke in. "Good thinking, Russ. There's no one in these parts who knows horses or their ailments better than Lee Varner. And that includes Doc Bell, who's a mighty good vet. Lee'll be able to keep an eye on Dusty for you if anybody can. Why, I've seen him pull horses out of pneumonia when everyone else thought they were dying.''

Dianne beamed at the praise Magnuson had for her father. If she suspected the real reason Russ wanted to have his horse at their place, she did not voice it. She told them she was sure her dad would keep the young gelding and check him over from time to time, but she would have to ask first. They loaded the hobbling quarter horse into Magnuson's trailer, and he put Dianne's Shadow in the second stall to take them both to Varners'.

As they got into the pickup Magnuson saw the concern in Russ's eyes and misread it as being entirely for his horse's welfare. ''Don't look so glum, Russ,'' he said, cheerily. ''I don't think Dusty's hurt all that bad. May not need any treatment, even from Lee. And you won't have any sweat getting to keep him over at Varners' till he's in shape again. That dad of Dianne's is a sucker for a good quarter horse. He's not goin' to turn him out.''

Russ relaxed slightly and, closing his eyes, he tried to pray. But, how could he pray when the thing he really wanted was for God to help him keep a lie covered?

Magnuson drove slowly through town and stopped at the Varner farm. ''Go in and talk to your dad, Dianne,'' he said. ''Then we'll take Dusty out to the barn and unload him and that Shadow of yours.''

The saddle club member knew Lee Varner well. He left the house at once and came out to the trailer to take a look at Dusty. He held the horse's left front foot off the ground and examined it.

''He took a nasty fall,'' he said. ''It's a good thing he didn't break his leg. That could easily have happened.''

Fear stabbed into Russ's heart.

"It's a bowed tendon," Mr. Varner retorted. "I wish we had a pasture to keep him in alone. He shouldn't be around other horses that would keep him running. He has to have a certain amount of exercise to keep circulation in his lower leg, but he'll have to be walked. You'll have to exercise him, Russ, but I'll keep an eye on him to see how he's doing."

When Russ got home an hour or so later his folks were waiting for him, wondering where he had been and why he was so late.

"I—I was helping Mr. Varner," he lied. "And when we got done I took Dusty out for some exercise. I'd hardly ridden him all week."

He kept his eyes averted as he spoke so his parents could not read the guilt that flecked them. He had to lie to them this time, he told himself. That was the only way he could keep from letting them find out where he had Dusty and what he had been doing all day. And that he had joined the saddle club without their permission. But it was not going to happen again. He would see to that.

His explanation seemed to satisfy his dad, who turned back to the newsmagazine he had been reading. But that was only for a moment. Mr. Masters put the magazine aside. "Didn't I see you walking across Varner's pasture just now?" he asked.

Russ nodded. "I always do," he replied.

"Where's Dusty?" Mr. Masters laughed good-naturedly. "Did you forget him over at the neighbor's?"

Crimson dotted the boy's cheeks. Now he had to lie again to cover up the other lies he had told. Would it *ever* stop?

"Yes," his mother broke in, "where is Dusty?"

He cleared his throat. "Mr. Varner thought he acted sort of dumpy, as though he was getting sick or something. He didn't have the life he usually has. So he told me I ought to leave my horse over at their place for a few days so he could give him some medicine and watch him.''

Mr. Masters frowned momentarily. "We certainly don't want him to get sick," he said. "He's a valuable animal, and he means a lot to you. I think I'd better phone Jay Bell and have him stop by and have a look at him.''

"Oh, no!" he exclaimed quickly. "Don't do that!"

His dad's eyes narrowed, questioningly. "I'd think you would want me to have Jay treat him, Russ. It's a lot easier for a vet to get hold of an illness in the early stages, than to wait." He got to his feet. "I'm going to call him.''

Russ panicked. "You can't call Dr. Bell!" he exclaimed.

"Why not?" By this time a note of suspicion had crept into Mr. Masters' voice.

"Mr. Varner won't like it," Russ said, defensively.

"That seems strange." He shook his head. "Why would he care? He should be as anxious as we are to have Dusty well again.''

The boy swallowed hard. "You see, it's this way. Mr. Varner has a thing about horses. He's worked around 'em so long he knows just about everything there is to know about taking care of them. When he saw that Dusty didn't look so good he said he would take care of him and give him medicine that would cure him. So, there's no need of having Dr. Bell, or anyone else look at him.''

"I know Lee Varner is one of the best horsemen in the state. I guess it stands to reason that he'd be able to take care of most of their ailments. But—keep a close watch on Dusty. If he looks as though he isn't improving in two or three days we'll have Jay go out and look at him. OK?''

The Masters boy sighed his relief. Excusing himself he

went into the kitchen and poured himself a glass of milk. A couple of times he thought he had been had, that his dad was catching him up in his conflicting reasons for not wanting him to call Dr. Bell to look at Dusty. The worst of all was when he used the excuse that Mr. Varner wouldn't like it if they called in the vet and his dad wanted to know why. He really sweat that one out. He was just lucky he had been able to find a reason for keeping Doc Bell out of it that had sounded halfway logical to his dad. With luck, he thought, the subject would not come up again.

Russ sat down at the kitchen table, his hand still trembling slightly on the glass. He had never before told one lie that took so many other lies to keep it covered up. Every time he was around his folks it seemed that he had to start lying to them to keep them from learning the truth about the things he had told them earlier. And each time he lied a white-hot iron was plunged deeply into his heart. What kind of a Christian was he, anyway?

When he got out of this mess, he promised himself, he would never lie again! There was not anything that could cause a guy more trouble than telling things that were not true! Especially to his folks, who trusted him and believed everything he told them just the way they had believed Chuck. The only difference was that Chuck had not let them down that Russ knew about. It seemed to him that *he* was always lying to them about something.

The following morning he got up an hour earlier than he usually did on Sunday morning and went over to the Varners' to see his injured horse. Dusty was standing in the stall placidly enough, but he favored his left front leg, holding it up slightly until it little more than touched the ground. Russ bent over to look at it, but he couldn't tell whether it was any better or not. The swelling seemed just about the same, but Dusty had been eating good. He thought that was an encouraging sign.

He took the young saddle horse out to the tank for water and had finished forking hay into the manger when Dianne came into the barn, concern clouding her pretty young features.

"How is he?" she asked.

Russ shrugged. "About the same, I think." He glanced down at the injured leg again. "I don't believe he's any worse."

"Dad seems to think it'll be several days before we'll know very much," she answered. "He was out to look at him last night after supper and again this morning as soon as we'd had breakfast. He doesn't think there's much to be done for an injury like this." She paused, smiling reassuringly. "But I just *know* that Dusty's going to be all right," she added. "He's *got* to be."

Russ stopped by the Varner place the next morning before the school bus went by. He could not really see much change in Dusty's leg, but he tried to make himself believe that it was better. Dianne insisted that she, too, could see a change.

Usually Monday's football practice was held to a light warmup drill and a discussion of the last game, almost play by play. This time, however, Coach Anson ordered the squad to suit up for a scrimmage.

"We won Friday night," he said, "but there's little for us to gain by going over a game like that one. I said we won, but that is not the whole truth. Oak Ridge came apart. They're a better football team than they showed us they were. Far better!" He stopped and looked about, searching the earnest young faces for some sign of arrogance or conceit. "We can't take credit for winning the game. Oak Ridge beat themselves. So forget all about last Friday night.

"The thing we've got to think about is the game we've got coming up this week. If we can beat Granby, our season has been a success. If we lose to them, it's been a failure. It's as simple as that."

Although Russ had played most of the last game, the following week the coach alternated him and Jerry Knoedler at quarterback. Jerry was at top speed and showed by his passing that the injury he suffered had not taken the edge off his skills. He could still execute the plays sharply and pass with deceptive ease.

Russ took charge a few minutes later and was able to keep the team going well enough, but there was an almost imperceptible difference. The plays were executed smoothly and his passes were well thrown and accurately placed, but something was amiss. He felt it, though he could not have explained what it was.

When he was directing them as quarterback the team went through the motions, mechanically, as though it was a job to be done. Each player carried out his assignment without error that afternoon, but again they were playing like so many robots programmed to certain skills. Those things they did and no more. With Jerry at the helm there was a spirit in them, a singleness of desire and purpose that helped them to function as a unit.

Russ was painfully aware of his own shortcomings as he left the field and stood quietly near two of the coaches. They continued their conversation without noticing that he was so close he could not have avoided overhearing them, even if he tried.

"I can't understand it," one of them was saying in low tones. "He walks like Chuck. He talks like Chuck. He even throws the football the same way Chuck did. But he sure isn't the football player Chuck was."

"Not by half," the other added.

Color stole into Russ Masters's cheeks, and he turned quickly away, not wanting to hear any more.

What the coaches said was all too true, he admitted to himself. He was Chuck's brother, but he certainly could not play football half as well as Chuck had—or basketball—or baseball—or track. Whatever he tried to do, the specter of his older brother's superior talents hung over him. He stared across the practice field at the hills that were reaching their treeless knobs upward to blot out the late afternoon sun.

There was nothing he would *ever* be able to do to win acceptance in Platte Valley. No matter what he tried, Chuck's accomplishments overshadowed his own puny efforts. That night at home he was unusually quiet, wrapped in his thoughts.

"What's the trouble?" his dad asked him. "Is Dusty worse?"

He shook his head. "Not that I know of. He seemed OK to me when I looked in on him this morning."

"Are you having trouble at school?" his mother wanted to know.

"Of course not," he retorted irritably. At least he was telling her the truth. He was not having the kind of trouble she was talking about.

"No papers to get in or tests coming up?"

He pulled himself erect, disgusted at her insistence that something was the matter. "No, Mom," he snapped. "I haven't got any tests coming up or any papers that are due and not finished. How many times do I have to tell you that?''

His dad flashed a quick warning with his eyes, and Russ fell silent once more. He should not have said what he did. He knew that. But they kept bugging him until he could hardly stand it.

All week Russ got up early enough to go over and see how Dusty was getting along. Tuesday he seemed about the same, but Thursday his lower leg began to swell around the hock and half to his knee. He seemed listless and dull of eye. There was still grain in the little box from the feeding before, and Dusty had only nibbled at the hay in the manger.

A knife stabbed into Russ's being as he rubbed the horse's warm nose and talked softly to him.

''He doesn't seem to be as good as he was, does he?'' Dianne asked from the doorway.

''What does your dad say about him?'' the boy asked with growing concern.

''That's what I wanted to tell you. Dad had to leave for Denver last night. He told me that we should watch Dusty closely, and if he seemed to be worse we should call Dr. Bell.''

Russ hesitated. He could not stand the thought of having Dusty sick, especially when he was getting worse. But he could not let his folks know that he had been lying to them, either. He knew they would be crushed and would be unlikely ever to trust him again.

''Think we ought to call the vet?'' Dianne asked.

He pulled in a thin breath and looked down at Dusty's swollen leg once more. For some reason it did not seem to be quite as swollen as it had been just minutes ago.

"Let's wait until tomorrow," he told her.

The next morning Dusty still had not eaten as he should, but his leg did not look much worse that he could see.

"I think I'll wait until tomorrow," he said. "If it hasn't started going down by then, we'll call Doc Bell."

Friday was the day of the Granby game. That was all the kids at school could talk about. There was a big rally that morning, and classes were to be dismissed at 2:30 so everyone would have a chance to get over to Granby by game time.

But Russ scarcely thought about the contest. His thoughts were fixed on Dusty and the leg that might be getting worse. Dianne was not going to the game. She seldom did. But that day she could not have if she wanted to. She was to go to the doctor with her mother, helping her out of the pickup and into the clinic building. There were hand controls on the vehicle, but she was not able to negotiate the steps without help that she could trust.

Dianne left school at noon on Friday and promised to look in on Dusty as soon as she got back to the farm.

She had not said anything about phoning him, but she did. He was still in the lunchroom when one of the secretaries came after him.

"Whoever it is said that it's an emergency," she told him.

"You'd better call Dr. Bell right away!" Dianne told him. "Dusty looks awful bad! He's lying down in the stall now. And I don't think he's eaten a thing all day!"

Russ's fingers trembled on the dial as he phoned the doctor after talking to Dianne.

"I'll be there in five minutes. Meet me in front of the school."

He slammed the receiver on the hook with unnecessary force and rushed out to the sidewalk in front of the building. He forgot the game and the fact that the team was to leave for Granby at 2:30 that afternoon. He forgot everything except his horse.

Dr. Bell examined the injured quarter horse carefully.

"You said he took a fall, didn't you?"

Russ nodded. "Stepped in a gopher hole." He expected the veterinarian to ask where and how it had happened, but he did not. He seemed to accept the fact that such things occurred and there was nothing anybody could do to avoid them. The boy was glad for that. It would help him to keep his parents from knowing the truth.

The doctor poked around at the swollen leg. "He's got a bowed tendon," he said. "But I believe we have another problem, too. His leg is hot and feverish, and he's running a temperature. I'd say he has infection. He must have punctured the skin above the hoof with a rusty nail or a piece of metal when he fell. It doesn't take much if conditions are right." He touched the swollen leg again, gently. "He's badly infected."

Russ looked down at Dusty. "Can you do something about it?" he asked. "I mean, he'll be all right, won't he?"

Dr. Bell smiled. "Now that we're treating him, I'd have to say he should be all right. Even without treatment he might make it. He's a healthy young horse. But now that we're taking care of him I don't think we have anything to worry about."

Russ knelt at Dusty's head, petting him and talking softly to him while Dr. Bell worked. It seemed to take hours to deaden the horse's lower leg, lance it, and clean out the wound, but of course it was only a matter of ten or fifteen minutes. At last he sewed up the gash he had cut, and looked up.

"I guess that does it, Russ."

"And he'll be OK?"

"As fit as rain." He grinned at him. "I'll give him a shot of penicillin today, and I'll stop by to see how he is tomorrow. Unless I'm badly mistaken it should begin to pick up by then."

He repacked his bag, and the two of them went to the car.

"I'm glad you called me when you did," he said "I'd hate to have missed that game tonight."

"Game?" Russ echoed. And then he remembered! The breath slammed out of him. "What time is it?"

"3:00. Why?"

"Oh, man! The team left for Granby half an hour ago! I was supposed to have been with them!"

"I wondered how you were able to go with me a little while ago. I know Chuck would have told me to go out and take care of the horse alone." He paused, thoughtfully. "Is there any place I can take you where you can catch them?"

"There's no chance of that now." He swallowed hard. "But I'd better go to my dad's office. I'll have to tell him what happened."

The veterinarian started the engine and whirled out of the yard toward town.

15

Dr. Bell swung over to the curb in front of Mr. Masters's law office and Russ got out, hurriedly. For a brief instant after the veterinarian pulled away the boy remained motionless, the chilled late October wind driving through his light sweater. He shivered and moved closer to the building.

Immense relief that Dusty was going to be all right swept over him, but that was overshadowed almost immediately by the blunder he had made. Missing the team bus to the biggest game of the season! He was sure that had never happened before in Platte Valley, and especially by a Masters. It was unthinkable!

Going in to face his dad was not going to be easy, he knew. He shuddered miserably at the confrontation that was evident. He already knew about what he would be told. "If you're going to play football, Russ, you've got to keep your mind on the game. Chuck would *never* have done what you did this afternoon. Even if he'd been so sick he should have been home in bed, he'd have dragged himself onto that bus and begged the coach to let him play. You know what is going to happen, don't you? Anson's going to kick you off the team, and I can't say that I would blame him!"

A talk like that would only be the beginning. His dad

would go on from there, ripping savagely into him until he felt like crawling under the furniture.

"Well," he told himself, starting for the door. "There's no need in putting it off any longer. I'd better go in and get it over with."

Hesitantly he stepped into the well-appointed reception room.

"Russell Masters!" the woman at the desk exclaimed when she saw him. "Where've you been? We've been phoning all over to find you!" The corners of her mouth tightened the way it used to when he was in her kindergarten class and she was about to reprimand him for talking or pulling the hair of the girl in front of him. "We've all been worried sick over you. I hope you know that."

His dad must have been listening from his private office. He came out then, concern darkening his handsome, finely chiseled features.

"Did Mrs. Varner tell you that we were trying to find you?" he broke in.

Numbly Russ shook his head.

"We were terribly worried about you," he went on, his voice taut with emotion. "When Coach Anson called to see if you were ill we couldn't imagine what happened to you. Mother was phoning from home, and Mrs. Peters and I were calling everyone we could think of from here. Then I remembered that your horse was sick, and I thought maybe you had gone out there to see about him. A call to Doc's told us we were on the right track."

Russ could feel his cheeks drain of color. The moment had come, and he was in for it. The blow was about to fall. His dad would not rip into him in front of Mrs. Peters. He was not that unkind. He would call him into the office and close the door. His voice would be so subdued anyone who happened to be in the outer office would be unable to hear what was being said. But that did not mean the ordeal would be any less devastating. And he should know. He had been through it more times than he liked to remember.

But Mr. Masters did not call him into his office as he expected. Instead he got his coat from the rack in the corner.

"Susan," he said to the receptionist, "call Melva and tell her that we'll swing by to pick her up." He strode toward the door. "Come on, Russ. We've got to hurry!"

Bewildered, his son followed him out to the car. "Where're we going?"

"To Granby to the game. Where else?

Russ hung back. "Coach Anson won't let me play," he announced firmly.

"Maybe not, but we'll never know unless we go, will we?"

At the house Russ got into the back seat so his mother could sit in front. He had really fouled things up by missing the team bus. He would never be able to live it down. He could hear the guys when he came to school Monday morning. And he could see the headlines in the sports section of the paper. CHUCK MASTERS'S BROTHER KICKED OFF TEAM. Coach Anson probably would not miss him all that much. He had Jerry Knoedler back, and he was doing a good job of handling the team. But he was sure he would never be forgiven for what he had done. Regardless of how the game came out the story would spread, and people would be down on him.

His folks had little to say on the drive to Granby. They visited casually, as though there was nothing amiss, talking about the nice fall they had been having, the snow that was predicted for the ski slopes of Colorado that weekend, and the activities at church.

He sat uneasily on the edge of the back seat. He wished his dad would jump on him about what he had done. It would make it easier if he did. But Mr. Masters remained silent about it. As they slowed at the city limits his dad glanced at his mother. "I'll go down to the locker room with Russ," he said. "When I come back we'll go and eat."

He parked near the Platte Valley school bus, and Russ and his dad got out. "I don't think this is a good idea," the boy said, nervously. "Coach Anson'll skin me. He'll skin me alive."

"When we've got a problem," Mr. Masters said without breaking stride, "the only thing to do is to meet it head-on."

When they entered the locker room the rest of the team was just beginning to suit up for the game. Coach Anson saw Russ and scowled angrily.

"What're you doing here?"

"Dad brought me over," he said, the cords in his throat tightening. "I'm sorry I missed the team bus."

The coach stopped what he was doing and came over to the boy and his father. "That's not good enough!" he exclaimed. "In all the years I've been coaching I've *never* had that happen before. It tells me that you really aren't interested in playing football."

"Russ has a good reason for not being on the bus," Mr. Masters began.

"Please, Dad!" he retorted, breaking in quickly. "This is my problem!"

His dad was about to go on, but stopped and stepped back. "I'm sorry, Russ. I shouldn't have interfered."

Anson's frown deepened. "All right, Masters!" he said, angrily. "Make it snappy. I've got a lot of things to do besides standing here listening to you alibi."

Russ was trembling by this time and sweat stood out on his forehead. "I—I don't have any alibi, coach. I blew it."

Anson's eyes narrowed curiously. "Go on."

"I—I'd like to suit up, but if you don't want me to, I'll understand. And if you kick me off the team, I'll understand that, too."

The coach picked up a towel from one of the benches and rubbed his hands as though to dry them.

"I shouldn't let you play again," he said. "It would only be fair to the rest of the squad who've been living up to our rules."

The boy nodded wordlessly.

"But you've come in here like a man and asked your dad not to interfere. And you haven't given me a lot of excuses for what you did. Now, I'm asking. Why did you miss the bus?"

He told him about his horse's being hurt and the phone call he got from Dianne telling him to get a vet to look at him. When he finished, the coach turned to the rest of the squad. "As soon as Russ goes out we're going to vote whether he stays on the team or not. OK?"

Mr. Masters touched his son on the arm and motioned toward the door. Outside, he turned to Russ. "I'm proud of you," he said, simply.

The boy raised his head to look at his father. It was the first time he had ever heard him say he was proud of him. He was still thinking about that when one of the guys came out and motioned him back inside.

"We took a vote," the coach said. "The team voted to let

you stay, so you can suit up if you want to. But I'm not saying you'll get to play tonight. In my book, if the game had meant anything to you, you'd have thought about it before you went running off to see about that horse of yours. Doc Bell could have taken care of him without your being there."

Russ nodded and began to unbutton his shirt, hurriedly. At least he was still on the team, even if he was not going to get to play. That meant a lot to him.

The temperature began to drop off that night shortly after the sun went down, and the wind switched to the north. It was a harsh, gusting wind that made both passing and punting completely unpredictable. Jerry handled the team well enough, but it was soon apparent that they were not up against a second Oak Ridge. Granby would not be rolling over and playing dead the first time they got hit. That proved to be exactly the way things were. In fact, the home team came out on the field ready for battle, and they fought Platte Valley for every yard.

The hometown team won the toss and elected to take the wind. Jerry stayed on the ground, moving the ball from the 20-yard line to their own 38 before having to kick on fourth and three. The kick was high and wobbly and was taken on the Granby 48, giving the home team excellent field position.

They knifed off-tackle for seven yards and registered a first in ten with a sweep around left end that had fans on their feet screaming for a touchdown. Only a desperation lunge by Platte Valley's safety drove the runner out-of-bounds. The next play was a short pass that was almost intercepted before going incomplete. The next was a hand-off that earned six yards and kept the sputtering drive going.

142

Early success gave Granby the impetus to keep moving, and they took the ball to the 12-yard line before a broken play sent the ball squirting away and Platte Valley recovered on their own 19.

The rest of the first half was a slugging match with the well-matched teams battling to score. Play was so hotly contested that both squads suffered an unusual number of injuries. Granby had a defensive end shaken up and lost two linemen to bad knees. And Platte Valley's offensive unit was badly hurt by injuries, particularly in the backfield. The wide receiver went out with a cracked rib and the two full-backs who alternated at that slot were sidelined. One had a broken nose, the other a pulled leg muscle.

Coach Anson began to look over the remaining backs. "You, Masters!" he called suddenly.

Russ knew what that meant and trotted over to him. "Yes, Coach."

"I wasn't going to use you tonight. You knew that, didn't you?"

He nodded solemnly.

"Letting you go in doesn't mean I approve of what you did."

"I know that, too."

"I just wanted to keep the record straight." His tone changed. "Have you ever played any backfield position other than quarterback?"

"A few times—in practice."

"And you know how to block?" They all had practice blocking. He was asking if Russ could block well enough to take the place of one of the injured men.

"Chuck and I used to practice blocking at home just for fun."

Coach Anson turned away to note the time left on the clock. There were four minutes remaining in the third quarter.

"OK. Go get 'em!"

Russ ran out on the field and joined the huddle. He was not in a position that counted for very much, he knew. About the only time anyone was aware of the guys doing the blocking was when one missed an assignment. Theirs was a job that was taken for granted. For some reason he thought of Chuck. He could not remember his brother playing at any other post than quarterback in a regular game. When the stats and the lineups came out in the paper on Monday, people would see them and be aware of the fact that he was not in Chuck's league and never had been.

As the play was called and they lined up on their own 31, a strange sensation swept over him. If Chuck had never played anywhere else beside quarterback, this was one game when Russ did not have anything to live up to. For the first time in his life he could go out on the field without having fans try to compare everything he did with the way his brother would have conducted himself. It was a free, relaxed feeling he had not known before.

The first play called for him to take out the defensive end to make a hole for Jerry Knoedler, who was to fake a hand-off and keep the ball for a wide sweep. He got a shoulder on his man and slowed him down enough to allow Jerry to make eight yards and a first down on the 39.

He did an acceptable job the rest of the third quarter and the first half of the fourth. Acceptable, but not outstanding. Then, with the ball on their own 27-yard line, third and seven, Russ threw a key block that sprung the runner into the flat. The ball carrier eluded a second tackler and faded to the sideline, where he picked up another block that let him turn the corner and scamper all the way to the Granby 2. The next play punched the ball in for the first TD of the night, giving Platte Valley, with the point after, a 7-0 lead.

Granby came roaring back on the kickoff return to their own 46-yard line. In a series of plays that used up four and a half minutes on the clock, they moved the ball across the midfield stripe to the Platte Valley 32 where the sustained drive faltered and came apart. Platte Valley took over on downs, and the offense came back on the field to assume the responsibility of eating up the final two and a fourth minutes on the clock. A fumble, then Granby came snarling back with a brief series of desperation plays that carried the ball inside the Platte Valley 10-yard line before the gun sounded, ending the game.

"You did a great job, Jerry," the fans called to the quarterback as the squad left the field.

Russ grinned. He doubted that anybody even saw the block he threw, but that did not make any difference. *He* knew about it.

When he got off the bus at the lane to his home he walked in slowly, wondering what his dad would say now. He was sure that he was thinking plenty. He probably had not said anything before because he had not wanted to get Russ upset before the game. Now, however, there was nothing to stop him. Hesitantly the boy made his way around the house to the back door. He wished there were some way of sneaking inside without being seen or heard, but there was not. Both his dad and his mom would be sitting there waiting for him.

16

Mr. and Mrs. Masters were sitting in the family room. He entered the room slowly, fumbling with the zipper on his jacket.

"I figured I'd better ride home with the guys on the bus," he said, lamely.

"That was fine. We understand."

He crossed to the fireplace and sat down on the raised hearth. For a time silence was heavy in the room.

"That was a great block you threw in the fourth quarter, Russ," his dad said after a few moments.

The boy's eyes lighted. "Did you see it?"

"See it?" Mr. Masters exclaimed. "It was the key block. If you'd missed him we'd have been thrown for a six or seven-yard loss, and the drive would probably have been stopped. As it was, you set Nelson free for the long run."

Russ glowed, but only for a moment. He was still sure that the axe would fall on him at any time.

"I have a feeling that Coach Anson will be moving you to fullback next week. That seems to be your spot."

He could not understand that. His folks had wanted him to take over where Chuck left off, and his brother had never played fullback. He was about to question it when his dad went on.

"We've done a lot of thinking tonight," he said. "Your mother and I."

"And a lot of talking about a lot of things," she added. "We've been doing you a terrible injustice, Russ. Will you forgive us?"

"Me, forgive you?" he said, incredulously. "I'm the one who blows everything. I ought to be asking you to forgive me."

"That's not true," his mother countered. "Dad and I got to talking about your horse tonight on the way home. You must love Dusty very, very much to have rushed out to Varners' with Dr. Bell to see what could be done for him. We've never seen that before, and we should have."

"That's right," Mr. Masters broke in. "To be honest with you, I resented Dusty and all the time you spent riding and taking care of him. All I could think of was that your horse was taking you away from time you should have been spending on football."

There was a long period of quiet when the only thing they heard was the loud ticking of the clock across the room. Russ had the idea that his parents were waiting for him to speak, but he could think of nothing to say.

"In our grief over losing Chuck," Mrs. Masters went on after a time, "we tried to make you over into a carbon copy of him. We reached the place where we expected you to be as good in sports as Chuck was, when God has obviously given you abilities and talents and interests in other things. And we expected you to take part in the same activities in church with the same exuberance that Chuck had."

He breathed deeply. "If I'd just worked hard enough at it I could have been the kind of quarterback you'd be proud of," he answered, his tone still blaming himself. "It's my fault."

"No," his dad said quickly. "It's not your fault. There isn't anything wrong with your being different than your brother. He was an outstanding Christian boy and a tremendous athlete. Probably the best our town has ever seen and will ever see for a long time. But that didn't make him any better or any more talented than you."

Russ started to contradict but remained silent instead.

"We should have realized this a long time ago—right after Chuck's death. I think we did, only we didn't want to admit it. But, going over this whole affair with Dusty today has made us see how wrong we have been. For the first time we've seen that we shouldn't have even wanted you to be like Chuck. God didn't make you like your older brother, and He didn't make Chuck the way He made you. You were two individuals with different personalities, different interests, and different talents and abilities. You couldn't be like Chuck, because God didn't make you that way."

His dad stopped, and in a moment his mother continued. "Where Chuck had a driving need to compete and win and the skills to do so in most team games, you have a love for horses and riding and being out-of-doors, Russ. Your interests and love are not better than Chuck's were. And his weren't better than yours. They're just different. This is what makes us feel so bad. We had not fully seen that until today. We were wrong in trying to make you like the same things Chuck did and try to do well in them. Terribly wrong. We must have put you through agony, Russ. Will you forgive us?"

His throat tightened. "It wasn't so bad," he muttered.

It was difficult for him to believe what was happening. He would have to talk to them several times in order to understand everything they were saying. Yet one thing got through to him—one thing he had never thought he would ever hear them say. It sounded as though they were no longer going to expect him to be as good as Chuck was in everything he did. He was going to be able to be himself. That was great. He felt as though a staggering load had been taken off his shoulders.

"There's something else we've decided," his dad said. "I know you like football. At least I hope you do, though whether you stay out for the team and go out next year is for you to decide. But we know your real interest is in horses and the rodeo team. I thought it was the most stupid thing I ever heard of to want to go out for rodeo when I thought you should be directing all your interest and attention toward football the way Chuck did. We were wrong about that, too. If you want to go out for the rodeo team we'll be there watching you the way we've been at all of Chuck's games."

Russ stared at him, hope and disbelief kindling at the same time in his eyes. This conversation had to be a dream. It could not be true! He would waken in a few moments to the same old hassle over the way he disappointed everybody.

"Only I don't want you to ride broncs or bulls, Russ," his mother said. "That's all I ask. The only thing I don't like about any of this is the chance that you might be hurt. If one of those brahma bulls threw you and stepped on you I think I'd die right in the stands."

He grinned at her. She was worried about his getting hurt. This was the real thing! It was not a dream. She had fussed about injuries every football season.

Russ and his parents had a wonderful time that night. They sat up until after one o'clock talking about Dusty and all that he planned to do with him. Still, there was one thing that suddenly drove its barbs into Russ's heart. He had lied to his folks, especially the last week or two. Not once, but many times. An inverted pyramid of lies. That he had joined the saddle club without their permission and allowed Dianne to get her dad's new hired man to sign for him were really more lies. And on top of them were the lies about Dusty's being sick when he actually had fallen at the fairgrounds while Russ was roping. Lies upon lies upon lies. And he was now a Christian! What was the matter with him?

Bitterness and remorse surged through his very being. He had such wonderful, understanding parents and how did he repay them? By lying!

He wanted to confess to his folks right then, to tell them what he had done, how sorry he was, and to ask their forgiveness. That was the only way he could have peace. The only way he could enjoy this change in his relationship with them. But how could he do that now? It would destroy any trust they ever had in him.

He told his mom and dad good night and went into his room, but he did not undress immediately. He was a believer in Christ. There was no doubt in his heart of that. But how could a Christian lie and be as deceitful as he had been? He dropped to the side of his bed and pulled off his cowboy boots.

Realization came slowly to him. He had been so frustrated and upset over trying to be like Chuck and failing so miserably that he got out of fellowship with the Lord. He neglected his Bible reading and prayer and found himself thinking about other things instead of listening in Sunday school and church. He had not given God the opportunity to speak to him and guide him.

He started to kneel beside the bed, but stopped and straightened slowly. He could not pray yet. He had something to do first.

His dad and mom were in their bedroom when he knocked on their door.

"It's awfully late, Russ," Mr. Masters said. "Can't it wait until morning?"

"No!" his voice was strained with emotion. "It'll only take a minute!"

They both came out into the family room with him and sat down.

"There's something I've got to tell you," he blurted. "Something I've done!"

They waited patiently.

"I wanted to join the saddle club so I could practice roping with their calves," he began, "but I knew you wouldn't like it so I joined without telling you." He went on to explain about the signature needed and that the new hired hand at Varners' had forged Mr. Masters's name. The only thing he left out was Dianne's part. He did not think it fair to risk causing trouble for her by revealing what she did. After all, it was for him. "From then on, it was one lie after another," he said, "as I tried to cover up what I had said before."

"That's the way it goes with lies," his mother observed. "One lie is seldom enough to cover a matter and each time we add a lie it gets a little easier for us to lie the next time."

"I'm really sorry that I didn't tell you the truth. Will you forgive me?"

"We have already," his dad replied.

They had a time of prayer together.

In the moments that followed a great refreshing wave

swept over Russ. And when he crawled into bed he dropped off to sleep immediately.

The next morning Russ left the house shortly after breakfast and went over to Varners'. Dianne was in the barn currying her horse.

"Dusty looks much better this morning," she said, excitedly. "You won't be able to ride him until that bowed tendon heals, but he's going to be all right."

He was glad to know that his horse was responding to treatment, but there was something else on his mind, something more urgent right then.

"I've got to talk to you, Dianne," he said, uneasily.

"Sure." She stopped what she was doing and faced him. "What about?"

"I—I had a long talk with my folks last night," he began. "I told them about joining the saddle club and getting your dad's hired man to sign the paper so I wouldn't have to go to my dad for his signature."

Her eyes widened. "You *what?*"

He repeated what he had said. "But I didn't involve you. I just told them who had signed the paper."

"Why did you do a dumb thing like that?" she demanded angrily. "Your folks would *never* have found out! It isn't as if you were going to be able to work out with us this fall. If you were, you'd be running the risk of someone telling them they'd seen you at the fairgrounds with the saddle club crowd.

"With that bowed tendon you won't be able to ride Dusty for several weeks, and then it'll be too cold. You had it made!" She was trembling with rage. "All you had to do is to keep your mouth shut!"

It was hard for him to continue, but he did. "Maybe I would've gotten away with it and maybe I wouldn't. That isn't the point. I'm a Christian now, Dianne. I've confessed my sin and have given my heart to Jesus Christ. I *had* to tell them. I had to get squared away with Dad and Mom—and with God." He paused and took a deep breath. "Of course I really couldn't have gotten away with it at all. God knew all about it."

"So. I might've known you'd tell them everything and get me into all sorts of trouble. But that doesn't matter to you, does it? I don't count!"

"That isn't the way it was at all," he countered. "I didn't tell them anything about you. I took the blame for everything."

She stared at him, her eyes flashing. "I don't know why you had to treat me this way," she said. "After everything we've done for you."

"I'm sorry you feel that way," he answered, "but I *have* to do what I feel is right."

Tears clung to her eyelashes. "Y-you can just take your horse back home," she said. "I know Dad won't want to keep him over here when he finds out what happened."

"I'll take him this morning. But I want you to know that your dad is not going to hear anything you did from me. And if he does find out I'll come over and take all the blame. It was my fault."

She eyed him in desperation for a moment, then whirled on her heel and fled to the house. He heard the door slam resoundingly behind her. He got his horse and led him out into the yard. He had had such plans for sharing Christ with Dianne. He had even worked out exactly what he would say and how he would say it. Somehow he had made himself believe that she would become a Christian, too.

It hurt to have her so angry with him and to realize that he wouldn't be able to talk with her about receiving Christ—at least until she got over being so mad at him. And he did not know when that would be. Weeks or months, maybe.

"Come on, Dusty," he said, starting slowly up the lane. "We'll just take it easy and you'll get there OK. Doc said you have to have some exercise, anyway."

His mind went back to Dianne. In spite of the way she exploded at him he was glad he had done what he had. For the first time he felt warm and clean inside.